Robert Bullock is a British SCBWI. Credits include *Noah Ramsbottom and the Cave Elves, Duck and the Moon Ghost, Learning Labs* and *Gerty Bendy Feet*, part of the poetry collection, *Crazy For Creatures: A Collection Of Animal Poetry*. Rob also writes for PETA's educational website. Current projects include a detective story for adults and an enthralling historical adventure for teenagers set in World War Two, *Jacob's War*.

Rob lives with his family in the Yorkshire Dales, with lots of animal friends, where he writes, plays the guitar badly and hopes to rescue more chickens, turkeys and maybe even the odd Llama if one needs a home!

Visit Rob's website at www.ninnylizard.com

SAM MARSH: The Viking King

By Robert J Bullock

Dedicated to my beautiful wife,

Kristen, for her patience,

support and love.

Copyright Robert J Bullock 2009

ISBN: 978-1-4452-1195-4

Publisher: Barklive Media, Norway.

Author Website: www.ninnylizard.com

Publisher website: www.thinkbank.me

CONTENTS

Prologue: Friday January 1st 1943, 11.11 am. Måsøy.

1) Friday October 15th 2011, 4pm. Grimwith Crescent.

2) Friday October 15th 2011, 4.11pm. Aircrash!

3) Friday 15th October, 8.11pm. Breaking News!

4) Friday 15th October, 9.21pm. Lofoten Islands.

5) 16th October 2011, 5.07am. Grimwith Crescent.

6) Saturday 16th October , 06.11am. Berlin.

7) 16th October, 08.30am. Grimwith Crescent.

8) 16 October, 10.15 am. Norway.

9) 16 October , 12.30pm. Yorkshire.

10) 16th October, 13.50pm. **Kurfurstendamm apartment.**

11) 16 October , 1pm. Leeds Airport.

12) 16 October, 13.05. Outside Leeds Airport...

13) 16 October , 1327pm. High over the North Sea.

14) 16 October, 13.41pm, The North Sea

15) Saturday 16th October, 15.30, Svolvaer.

16) 16 October, 16.00, Helipad.

17) 16 October, 17.00 The Royal Villa, Svolvaer. Settling in.

18) 16 October, 17.30 Neuwerk, boarding the X boat.

19) 16 October, 21.00pm. Grandma arrives.

20) 16 October, 22.30 pm. Deep beneath the North Sea.

21) 16 October, 22.57 pm. Bridge of HMS Vigilant

22) 17 October, 1.00 am. X boat 1A

23) 17 October, 9.00 am. The Royal Villa, breakfast.

24) 17 October, 13.00. Surprise visitors!

25) 17 October, 14.00 Unterwasserwelt.

26) 17 October, 14.30. Royal Villa with friends.

27) 17 October, 18.00.The bridge of Unterwasserwelt.

28) 17 October, 18.10. RFS Alexander Nevsky.

29) 17 October, 21.00. Sat in the lounge of the villa.

30) 18 October, 10.30. Alfie Blom

31) 19 October 8.00 am.Diving with Alfie Blom.

32) 19 October, 12 noon. Unterwasserwelt.

33) 19 October, 12.05.On board the DSV.

34) 19 October, 14.30. Bad Atlantic storm.

35) 19 October, 16.30. Unterwasserwelt arrives.

36) 19 October, 20.00 hours. Royal villa.

37) 19 October, 2030. Ramsund Special Forces Base.

38) 19 October, 21.00. The Royal Villa.

39) 19 October, 21.46. The gardens.

40) 19 October, 22.30. Rocket Sofa's!

41) 19 October, 22.45. The Røst Reef

42) 20 October, 02.00. The Royal villa.

43) 20 October 6 am. Unterwasserwelt.

44) 20 October, 6.10. The surface above the Røst Reef.

45) 20 October, 6.25. The Bridge.

46) 20 October, 6.35. The Royal villa.

47) 20 October, 6.45. The Bridge.

48) 20 October, 7.15. The Villa.

49) 20 October, 8.20 am. The big stick.

50) 20 October, 8.25. The Royal villa.

51) 20 October, 9.05. Unterwasserwelt.

52) 20 October, 10.00 am. The Remains

53) 20 October, 11.00 am. USS Theodore Roosevelt.

54) 20 October, 12 noon. Deep beneath the sea.

55) 21 October 2011, 10 am. Alfie Blom's cottage

Prologue: Friday January 1st 1943, 11.11 am. The village of Havøysund, on the island of Måsøy.

"The technicians report that the seals have ruptured because of the cold, sir!" reported the chief scientist, Professor Jahnke who was starting to develop icicles from his nose. Here close to the village of Havøysund, it was minus 30 degrees Celsius. The village is located deep within the Norwegian Arctic Circle on the island of Måsøy, not far from the Northern Cape, the most northerly part of mainland Europe. It was the perfect place to avoid the prying eyes of the British, the Americans and even the Russians that inhabit the islands a few hundred miles to the south west. Up here experiments could be conducted in total secret and this was a top secret project.

"Test it anyway!" replied the young Sturmbannführer Eric Krater.

Krater was a high flying SS Officer who had formerly been a professor of physics at Berlin's oldest university, the Humboldt.

For some academics the war had been a major interruption to their research but to Krater it had given it an unexpected boost, funds were freely available and he could go wherever he wished to conduct his tests. His work on non solid fuel rocket propulsion was getting really exciting. By developing a way of creating anti matter in his laboratory he was making science fiction science fact. Sure it was an unstable fuel but its possibilities were almost limitless. Krater was most interested in how it could power vast rockets at almost light speed. If his work bore fruit the war would definitely be over within six months. The Fatherland would literally obliterate the enemy without them even being able to fire a shot in defence! He'd even spoken to the Führer himself about his plans and he was so excited he'd given him almost unlimited funding for his work.

"But Herr Sturmbannführer!" argued the scientist, "it's too dangerous for the pilots!"

"There is no risk," smiled Krater calmly, "no risk at all, trust me. Be a good scientist and start the countdown, Jahnke."

"Very well, Herr Sturmbannführer," he picked up the radio and spoke to the control room, "prepare for launch!"

Two minutes later the control room replied to Profesor Jahnke, "All systems operational Professor, ready for countdown."

"OK, zehn, neun, acht, sieben, sechs, fünf, vier, drei, zwei, eins, gehen!"

Through a huge hole in the ground about two kilometres from where they stood there was a loud hissing, then there was a massive amount of vibration that seemed to shake the whole island. Suddenly a sleek, tall skyscraper of a rocket catapulted out of the hole high into the northern sky in complete silence.

"It works!" shouted Krater triumphantly holding his fists high into the freezing air, "I knew there was no problem with the seals!"

Even as he was still celebrating, high up in the sky, the rocket started making a lot of noise, vibrating terribly and then in a blinding flash it exploded, completely vaporising as it shot into space at almost the speed of light.

On the ground Professor Jahnke took a deep breath and headed inside to get warm. Krater remained frozen to the spot staring high into the sky in disbelief.

1) Friday October 15th 2011, 4pm, Garden Shed, 22 Grimwith Crescent, Holmford, England - Flying machine!

"I bet you it won't even get off the ground!" grunted Spike Williams who was bored and hungry, Spike was always hungry.

"Yeah it will!" declared Sam Marsh defiantly, "It will because I've followed the instructions *precisely*," Sam Marsh was an avid inventor, he was interested in how things work. His favourite kind of day would be one where he went to his shed and took a load of things to pieces. Now he was pretty good at putting them back together properly but when he was younger he just put them back together, not at all properly.

"Yeah, whatever! Anyway I'm off for something to eat," mumbled a disinterested Spike as he turned to go.

"You'll be lucky" sneered Jenny James as Spike disappeared out of the shed and up the garden path, mumbling to himself.

"What do you think, Jen?" asked Sam. He always valued what Jenny thought on almost every subject.

"Well, you did follow the instructions to the letter, didn't you?"

"Yeah!"

"But I'm just not sure about that website, Sam, it's got all sorts of rubbish on it. I mean who's ever heard of rocket candy?"

"What do you mean?"

"Well, think about it? If someone could invent a flying chair fuelled by sweets then don't you think we'd all be bobbing about in them?"

"Dunno," grunted Sam.

"Think about it, Sam. Someone would be making money out of it!" Jenny was sensible, a tomboy type of girl, really strong and intelligent. Sam knew what she said always made sense. "But Rocket candy is real, here take a look when I google it, look, there's loads of websites about it, it's well known to us inventors."

"Oh Sam," said Jenny, she thought Sam was gullible. He was so keen to invent things, especially things that would fly, Sam had a thing about being able to fly.

"Let's try it at least," said Sam hopefully. Sam Marsh had been an inventor since he was little. He'd always built stuff since he was a tiny boy, he started with plastic Lego, then Meccano from kits, then he moved on to small machines and motors that he'd find in skips or in the garbage. He was good at it too. Now he was anyway, though Jenny could tell some good stories about when Sam wasn't very good at it. TV's that whirred like washing machines and washers that picked up TV signals! Satellite dishes that tuned into the space shuttle as it flew over instead of the Sky satellite.

But Sam had learned a lot from his mistakes and now he could repair hoovers, hairdryers, just about anything you cared to put in front of him. People from up and down the estate would bring him their appliances when they conked out and Sam always fixed them. Quite often someone would knock on their door after school or on a Saturday morning asking for Sam to repair some curling tongs or fix a CD player. Sam always managed to fix whatever they brought and people always gave him something for his troubles. Mrs Lowes from down the road had chickens so she paid him in fresh eggs. Old Mr Styles was a model maker and used to give him unfinished model cars so Sam could put a tiny motor in it and use a remote control. Sam loved being an inventor.

"OK, why not," said Jenny.

Sam and Jenny opened the shed door and carried the modified old arm chair that they'd found in a skip out into the small overgrown council-house garden. Attached to each of the stumpy legs were large, shiny metal tubes. On the right arm was a joystick and on the left arm was a big red button. On the back of the chair were two silver tanks that looked like diver's air tanks.

"Er! It's raining!" said Jenny rushing back to shelter in the shed.

"Rain's good Jenny!" said Sam, "It'll stop any fires!"

Sam, put an old motor bike helmet over his head, closed the visor and pulled on a pair of thick gardening gloves he'd found. He sat down in the arm chair and buckled up an old belt Jenny had stitched into the chair.

"You ready?" shouted Jenny loudly.

"Ready!" called back Sam in a muffled voice.

"OK I'll count down then!"

"Right!"

"OK," said Jenny, " Three...two....one....blast off!"

Sam braced himself and pressed the red button firmly. There was a loud gurgling sound as the substances in the tanks started mixing together.

"Ssssssss" loud hissing noises were coming out of the silver tubes on the legs, "Pffffffff" the noise was getting louder and louder. Suddenly, the gases ignited and powerful flames were coming out of the tubes, scorching the soaking wet grass. Gradually the chair lifted off the ground, one centimetre, five centimetres, fifteen, fifty. One metre, two meters. It felt like Sam was flying! Suddenly the power cut out and the chair crashed to the ground with a heavy thud.

"Sam, Sam! Are you alright?" cried Jenny as she rushed to the chair.

She pulled Sam's helmet off and was met with Sam's grinning face!

"Sam!"

"I flew, I flew the chair! Did you see it Jenny? I flew the chair!"

"Yeah! You flew! I saw it! You flew!"

Sam was so excited, "I know I need to fine tune the sugar/potassium nitrate mix but at least I got it off the ground! That's the main thing! The rest is just fine tuning!"

2) Friday October 15th 2011, 16.11 local time, West Coast of Norway - Air Crash!

Captain Belloch expertly pulled on his sky diving suit and parachute. Firmly buckled in, he bent down and emptied all the other parachutes from the store and kicked them towards the door. Bracing himself, Belloch slowly opened the outer door. Suddenly a violent rush of freezing air enveloped him as the cabin decompressed. Belloch had to use all his strength to struggle to stay by the door. He was being sucked out before he was ready to jump. But he had one last thing to do. Looking down he could see that two parachutes had gone already, dragged out into the night air. Quickly, he kicked the others out behind them. Then, steadying himself, he checked his watch one final time and, grinning evilly, leapt out.

The Cessna Citation luxury private jet was juddering violently from the decompression and was starting to drop from the sky like a stone. In the cabin all the passengers were thrown violently forward. One passenger gashed his head badly and blood was spurting everywhere.

Quickly, co-pilot James Smithers, who had been sat talking to the passengers, regained his composure and made his way to the front of the plane. He desperately tried to get into the cockpit but couldn't as it was deadlocked from the inside. In a panic, Smithers clambered to the rear of the plane where the two stewardesses were struggling frantically to try and pull the rear door open.

"It's locked from the inside!" shouted Sue Archibald, "It must have been Belloch!"

"Here, let me try!" shouted Smithers, but it was no use. The door was deadlocked in some way like the other.

The plane was dropping from the sky like a lead weight and there was nothing anyone could do to stop it.

"Everyone assume emergency position!" shouted Smithers taking a seat and buckling himself in. But he knew it would be no use. There was nothing anyone could do. They were headed straight into a rocky mountain at the side of a Norwegian fjord!

3) Friday 15th October 8.11pm 2011, 22 Grimwith Crescent, Holmford, England - Breaking news.

"We are just interrupting this programme to bring you a news flash!" said the television announcer who had just interrupted Jessie Brooks' favourite tv quiz show, Big Bonanza Bingo.

Jessie Brooks was addicted to bingo, she absolutely loved it, it was everything to her. She lived and breathed bingo. It was her entire sad life. She went out to play it every night. Even when she was sick she struggled to crawl to the bingo hall. She spent all the money on gambling that she was given for her foster children. Jessie never won but that didn't stop her, no, on the contrary, it made her even more eager to play! Each evening she would get drawn into the heady anticipation of bingo and pints of sweet cider and each morning, as she woke up the worse for wear, she wished she hadn't.

"Oh no, just my luck," she wailed pathetically from her armchair in which she wedged her massive, flabby bulk for almost every waking minute she didn't play bingo, "he was about to call house! He was! That man! The one with the bow tie! Did you see him Jenny? Did you? Spike? Sam?" Jessie

Brooks was always keen to share what she considered to be the wonder that is bingo with everyone else, "He was about to shout, he was, I saw it with my own eyes!"

"As opposed to seeing it with someone else's?" said Jenny, curtly, not bothering to look up from her book, "No, I wasn't watching, so I didn't see him Jessie."

It was a history book that she was so caught up in. Jenny was really interested in history. Her current book was a book about the battle for the Russian city of Stalingrad in the Second World War. To most people, especially to most kids of her age, this wouldn't be their preferred reading matter, but to Jenny it was pure gold. She loved history. She immersed herself in it.

Jenny was eleven. Tall and skinny, and freakishly strong, she was tougher than most boys at least two years older than her. She had perfect white skin and huge amounts of frizzy red hair that she tied back. No one ever messed with Jenny James! Not if they liked keeping their nose in the middle part of their face that is! Sean Driver had been the last unfortunate person to feel the weight of Jenny James' fist and now there's a stretch of wall just by the main girls' toilets at Holmford High School that will forever have a red tint!

"What about you Spikey!" asked Jessie hoping that Spike was enjoying Big Bonanza Bingo as much as she was.

To Jessie, Big Bonanza Bingo was as good as life got outside an actual bingo hall, it combined the most amazing thing ever invented, bingo, with the ability to sit in a comfy armchair and get everyone to bring her cup after cup of sugary tea and packet after packet of cheesy puffs, which were her favourite food!

But instead, Spike was playing furiously on his most prized possession, his game boy. All you could see when he was hunched over playing on it was a mop of wild blond hair. Spike got his nickname "Mop" from his unruly hair.

"Urgh!" grunted Spike in a feeble attempt at communication in actual language. Mop was completely caught up in his game.

"Oh, never mind!" mumbled Jessie, "Don't mind me! I'm Miss Nobody! Nobody, nobody! I might as well be called the invisible woman!" Jessie was ranting, "Never mind me, I'm just the one who puts food on the table and clothes on your backs!"

"In your dreams!" said Jenny under her breath. Jenny, Sam and Spike shared out the cooking and shopping duties as best they could. They were self sufficient kids, it was either that or starve!

"Can you put the sound back on please, Jessie? It might be interesting," said Sam who was sat beside Jenny on the sofa reading a book about submarines and daring special forces operations. Sam had become interested in these techno-thrillers after his school librarian, Mrs Eaton, had told him about them. Her husband had been a Royal Marine and when she told Sam about some of his exploits and then that there were plenty of books with exciting stories like that Sam had devoured the first story and then all the ones he had read after that. Mrs Eaton always made a fuss of Sam, and because no-one else had ever done this, Sam really savoured his trips to the library. Mrs Eaton always ordered the books Sam liked and kept them to one side.

"Oh, alright!" chuckled Jessie, "You're a right clever clogs, you are, Sam Marsh, I just hope I don't miss too much of the action. Come on dogs, out you go, you lazy old beggars," Jessie struggled to heave herself slowly out of her chair and started waddling out of the room, followed by two sleepy black greyhounds, she was still mumbling about the bingo, "tutt! And it was just starting to get good it was too. Bloomin' TV news flashes! I'll flash them!"

Sam and Jenny snorted and burst into fits of laughter at the thought! Jessie was oblivious, her mind completely devoted to her goal of the kitchen cupboard with the sweet cider in it.

Sam Marsh had just turned twelve. He was an orphan who had no idea who is mum and dad were. In fact he was dumped when he was just a small baby. Sam Marsh wasn't even his real name, it was just a name that the person who had found him gave him. He shook his head, tutted to himself and reached for the remote to turn up the volume.

"Just to remind you of the reason for this newsflash," said the serious looking newsreader, "a Norwegian news agency is reporting that a private Cessna jet plane crashed this evening on the west coast of Norway. It is understood that several members of an ancient Norwegian aristocratic family were on board the plane. Although details are sketchy, initial reports are suggesting that there is little or no chance that there are any survivors of the crash. One eye witness report has said that the plane exploded upon impact. Well, that's all for now, you can, of course get more on this story as it develops over on the news channel, and we will bring you further details in the news at ten. Now, we are returning you to Big Bonanza Bingo."

"All dead!" said Sam quietly under his breath. He felt really upset by the news of the accident, felt that he actually knew the people who had died. He knew this was ludicrous and he couldn't put his finger on why he felt like he did. He just felt a strange sense of loss like he would if anything happened to Jenny or Spike. For Jessie, not so much!

"All dead!" mumbled Sam to no-one in particular.

"Yeah, that's terrible news, terrible," answered Jenny not looking up from her book.

Sam sat quietly for a few moments then realised the programme was back on.

"Jessie!" he called out, "Jessie! Are you there? Big Bonanza Bingo's back!"

"Tell 'em to wait Sam," called Jessie from the bathroom, "I'm coming, I'm coming, I'm coming!"

4) Friday 15th October 2011, 9.21pm local time, west of the Lofoten Islands - Discovery of The Helmsfjord.

Thud! The mini sub stalled violently as it unexpectedly hit something solid. It revved its motors furiously but it felt like it was in the tight clutches of some unknown sea creature that lurked deep in the bleak northern ocean.

For over three days now the two man sub had dived deeper and deeper off the western coast of Norway. It was scouring the sea bed metre by metre, searching for something. Now it needed every bit of its immense bulldozer like strength to free itself from the sea's clutches.

The powerful motors buzzed away, propellers first going clockwise, then anti clockwise, backwards and forwards, until the machine started to rock from side to side and gradually struggled free from the cold water reef.

Gingerly, it inched slowly forward off the jagged edges of the living reef. It then continued its painstakingly slow work of systematically scouring every bit of the sea bed off the great northern reef that lies just off the coast of the Norwegian Lofoten Islands.

"I think I see something!" said a harsh voice in Russian.

"Where? I can't see anything," argued a second man squinting through the steamed up thick glass portholes, "it's nothing."

"It's not nothing! There! Look! Look!"

"Where?"

"Open your eyes man!" He was pointing with grubby hands, "That's clearly the hull of something, maybe a ship or a sub. And if we can pull around we can look for identification."

"OK, pulling around."

The mini sub used its impressive agility to get a closer look at the side of the wreck.

"There it is! I think I can see a name!"

The man peered harder through the murky water that was being churned up by the sub's propellers and in the spot lights from the sub some letters became visible.

"It's upside down," said the older man, "and it is a sub. Wait! I think I can just make out the letters. Wait! All stop!"

The sub used forward thrust to bring it to a complete halt.

"What is it Sir?"

"Er, it's difficult to make out, no, I think I've got it...H, E, L," He spelled out the letters slowly, "the middle ones aren't too clear. No that's it! Got to be! Helmsfjord, Helmsfjord. It's her! We've found her. She's been sleeping down here for all these years with the key to a trillion dollars and control over the entire world locked in her vault."

As he turned to grin triumphantly at the other man, his mouth opened to reveal a disgusting set of rotting brown teeth, that stunk so bad it made the other man gag violently.

"But Sir, it's right underneath the reef itself," answered the second man, putting his hand over his nose and mouth.

"Niet, Niet, don't worry your tiny little brain Misha, it sure won't worry Herr Krater. That ship is the key to his plans!"

"But the reef?" argued Misha.

"Hey! Misha, Misha," soothed the older man, "believe me, the reef is not a problem!" cackled Brownteeth.

"But surely it will stop Krater's teams of divers getting at the wreck?"

"Do you think so, Comrade?" The brown-toothed man, turning, stared straight into his colleague's eyes. His face was gnarled and hideously pock marked and his cheeks looked as if some dreadful disease was eating away at him from inside.

His acid breath blew directly onto Misha's skin making him cringe and back away, "Now listen to me Misha. I know Herr Krater well, as well as anyone alive, maybe too well, I don't know. But I've seen him do terrible things, things I will never speak of and, for what's buried in that ship, believe me, Krater will pull apart this reef with his bare hands if needs be!"

5) 16th October 2011, 5.07am, 22 Grimwith Crescent - The Visitors.

Thud, thud thud! Ring, ring, ring! Thud, thud, thud! Someone wanted to speak to the inhabitants of 22 Grimwith Crescent really urgently.

"Alright! Alright!" yelled Jessie Brooks from her bed as the visitors threatened to drag her from her drunken stupor with their knocking, she'd only got to bed at midnight after rolling in from playing bingo with her cronies, "Jenny, Sam, Spike!" she called but no-one answered, "Oi!!" she yelled at the top of her voice, "God help me! Will *someone, anyone* get that bleeding door! My head's thumping bad enough without some idiot adding to it!"

Thud, thud thud! Ring, ring, ring! Thud, thud, thud! Whoever it was, they were relentless. It had to be something serious.

Sam reached out for his bedside light, fumbled about a bit and eventually managed to switch the lamp on, which momentarily blinded him. He grabbed his clock and checked the time.

"It's 5 am!" he mumbled at Spike who was still snoring, but not even a bomb dropping on the house could wake up Mop! Sam had a theory that it was all the hair he had that muffled sound so well. One day he would conduct an experiment, thought Sam, it could benefit people all around the world, he would sell the secret of Spike's amazing, sound muffling hair! He'd make an absolute fortune, millions and millions.

Sam crawled out of bed and put his dressing gown on.

"Kids!" shouted Jessie pathetically, "*Please I'm begging you!* Is *anyone* going to get the bleedin' door?"

"Alright, alright! I'm going, keep your wig on!" snapped Jenny who met up with Sam at the top of the stairs.

"Who on earth can it be at 5 o'clock, Jen?" asked a worried Sam.

"No idea," replied Jenny looking worried too, "but whoever it is, they want to speak to someone really badly."

"But surely that can't be a good sign, can it?"

"No, I wouldn't have thought so Sam."

Jenny peeked through the spy hole and then turned to look at Sam.

"Two men," she said, "two men in dark suits."

Sam slipped the chain across, opened the door a fraction and peered through cautiously.

"Samuel Marsh?" asked one of the men, who was dressed in a black suit with a black tie.

"Err, who wants to know?" replied Sam suspiciously.

"OK," the man was checking something in a file, he turned to his colleague, "we have a positive ID, Svend."

"What are you talking about, positive ID?" asked Sam.

"Sam, we need to speak with you urgently," said the other man, who looked a lot younger than the first.

"What do you want with him? Who are you?" asked Jenny from firmly behind the door.

"Oh, I'm sorry," replied the younger man, "my name is Svend Erstad and this is Odd Aukland."

"Those are strange sounding names," said Sam.

"They're Norwegian names Sam, we're from the Norwegian secret service." said Odd, "Look, this is important, we need to speak with you really urgently Sam, can we come in, please?"

"Oh, I've had enough of all this," snapped Jenny about to slam the door shut, "why should we believe what you say?"

suddenly she stopped speaking, "Oh, I know, ID, yeah, we need to see your ID's."

"Oh, yeah, sure, sorry," said Odd, "no problem".

Each of the men passed their personal ID cards through the tiny gap in the door and, exactly as the men had said, they were from the Norwegian secret service.

"Look, is your guardian available? We really need to speak with you urgently," asked Svend.

Just at that moment a small car pulled up outside the house and Sam's case worker from social services, Sarah Steel, hurriedly got out and rushed up the path.

"Mrs Steel?" asked Svend reaching out to shake her hand.

"Mr Aukland and Mr Erstad?"

"Yes." replied Svend.

"Sam and Jenny, is that you?" asked Sarah peeking through the gap in the door.

"Sarah?" they replied together.

"Yes, it's me."

"Oh," sighed Jenny, "are we glad to see you!"

"I'm sorry I'm late. Where's Jessie, still in bed?"

"Yeah," replied Jenny.

"There's a surprise! Come on, let us in and we'll try and get to the bottom of this," said Sarah as Sam unlocked the door and let them in, "it's very important."

The two Norwegians and Sarah didn't see the men crouched in the beaten up old Ford Escort van across the road from 22 Grimwith Crescent. Sat in total darkness the men had arrived just minutes before Odd and Svend. They'd seen the two men in black suits arrive in a black Mercedes car and bang on the door until it had opened just a crack. They'd seen a flustered looking woman pull up and rush up the path. They'd seen them all go inside.

One of the men made a solitary telephone call using a scrambler device on a special satellite cell phone, in a foreign language, then they drove away.

"Look, I know this is a lot to take in Sam," said Svend sitting on the sofa as Jenny passed him, Odd and Sarah each a cup tea.

"You're telling me!" snapped Sam pacing about, " One minute I'm this deadbeat kid nobody wants, living in a foster home on a rotten estate in Holmford and the next you're telling me my real parents were the king and queen of the Lofty Islands!"

"They weren't the king and queen, Sam," corrected Odd quietly, "and they're the Lofoten Islands,".

"Whatever!" snapped Sam who continued ranting, "Some Islands with a strange name somewhere near the North sodding Pole!"

"Well, it's not that near the North Pole, Sam," said Odd, ignoring the swearing. Although it didn't go unnoticed by Sarah Steel who raised an eyebrow at Sam which didn't go unnoticed by Sam!

"It is actually in the Arctic Circle though, Odd," argued his colleague.

"And," continued Odd ignoring his colleague, "they were not actually called King and Queen, Sam. Your father and mother were the Chieftains."

"Well from King and Queen to Chieftains is not that big a jump is it?" Sam stared at Odd, "But from foster son of Blobby Blobberson here in this dive to living in a villa, now that's something else!"

Sarah and Jenny weren't surprised that Sam wasn't taking the news about his parents too well. They knew Sam felt truly betrayed by his real parents. He'd talked about it enough. And now this. If they had been sick or really poor Sam could have understood them abandoning him, they would have had a good reason and would have been trying to give him some sort of better life. But getting rid of your baby when you live in palace, with millions and millions of pounds, or kroner, in the bank! No, he couldn't ever forgive that! There could be no reason to abandon your child when you were almost royalty. Sam was so angry that he'd failed to hear that Odd had said *were*, not *are*.

Sam, who'd gone red in the face and had tears in his eyes, turned to Odd and Svend, "Well, they can't have me back! Not now! Not after all these years! They can't just send two men over and take me from my home just because they feel like it now!" Sam stood up and started pacing the room, "I mean, I know this place is a dive and all that, but it's home, the only one I've got, the only one I've ever had," Sam gave the Norwegians a bitter stare, "and at least I've got my friends here."

"Er Sam," said Jenny quietly, she'd started piecing the bits of the story together, "Sam!"

"Mm, yeah," said Sam not really listening.

"Sam!"

"What?" She'd got his attention.

"Sam, I think there is something else the men have come to tell you."

"What?"

"About your parents."

"Er, yeah, thanks Jenny," said Odd quietly, "there is something else Sam, two things actually, important things that we have to tell you."

"What else can there be?" snapped Sam bitterly, glaring at the men, who he was getting increasingly angry with, "I don't know if I want any more surprises."

"Sit down Sam, please," begged Sarah, reaching out for him and pulling him towards her.

"Sam," said Svend gently, "your parents are dead."

"What? Dead?" Sam was stunned, "What? Where? How?"

"Maybe you heard about the accident on the news? It's been on all the channels. They died in a plane crash yesterday evening."

"Crash?"

"Yes, they died yesterday evening, their plane crashed into the side of a fjord."

"Crash? *That* crash?" Sam was remembering the newsflash that interrupted Jessie's Big Bonanza Bingo, "That was *them*? My mum and dad?"

Sam slumped on the sofa next to Sarah, he didn't know what to think. Five minutes ago he'd been given his parents back and the now they'd been snatched away from him in the most cruel way possible. Sam had felt angry at first, resentful towards them for giving him away, leaving him on a door step, and now he was starting to feel guilty about the things he was thinking and saying.

"I'm afraid it's true Sam," added Odd.

"But there's something else too," said Svend.

"What else?" Sam was miles away, thinking about his dead parents who he'd had just for a few minutes.

"I don't know how to say this Sam," said Svend, "it's just that.."

"Yeah, I'm listening," this was only partly true, Sam was still miles away.

"Sam, you're the only child that the couple had."

"The only child? You mean I don't have any brothers and sisters?" Now they'd got Sam's full attention.

"No, none" continued Svend, "So, the thing is Sam, now you are their legacy!"

"What?"

"What I suppose I'm trying to say is, Sam, that now you're the new Chieftain of the Islands of Lofoten!"

"What?"

"Sam," continued Odd, "it's true. You're now the new Chieftain of Lofoten! A Viking King you could say! You've got to come home to your people. They need you."

6) Saturday 16th October 2011, 06.11am. Berlin local time, exclusive top floor Kurfurstendamm apartment.

The phone on the large antique French oak desk rang only once, the call was expected, the man picked up the phone.

"Sprechen Sie?"

"Herr Krater," said a German voice, "they have arrived."

"How many are there?"

"Two from the secret service plus an English woman."

"An English woman?"

"Ja."

"And they have entered the house?"

"Ja, Herr Krater."

Krater was silent for a moment. He was thinking very carefully about his next move, he was a chess grandmaster, for him real life mirrored his favourite game and he never lost at chess.

"Herr Krater, Sir?"

"Ja, ja, everything is as I expected, as I have planned. OK, fall back to a position well away from the house but continue to monitor the house using the electronic surveillance you installed."

"Ja, Sir."

"But remember, you must not be detected! Got it?"

"Ja, Ja, got it Herr Krater."

"Now listen to me. I want to know when they plan to travel to Norway, understand?"

"Ja, Sir!"

"You will allow them to take off but they must not be allowed to make it to their destination, got that?"

"Ja, Herr Krater, we will organise the elimination of the boy."

Krater replaced the phone and stood up. He wandered slowly over to the window and watched the first signs of daylight dawn over the exclusive street of Kurfurstendamm in the German capital city of Berlin. From his bird's nest he could see all the exclusive stores, restaurants and hotels.

He'd been surprised when he'd discovered that there was a child, his intelligence reports had been wrong. Krater did not tolerate anyone giving him wrong information and he'd dealt swiftly with them. But he'd re-gathered his thoughts quickly, as in chess he'd had to respond to the unexpected move of an opponent. The child was merely a minor irritation. Soon he, Krater, and The Company would control everything. He started laughing quietly.

"The Chieftan is dead!" he muttered, chuckling to himself.

7) 16th October 2011 08.30am, 22 Grimwith Crescent.

"Would you like ketchup with your scrambled eggs Odd?" asked Jenny as she dished out a plate of eggs to the chubby Norwegian. In all the time that Svend Ersand had known him Odd Aukland had never turned down the offer of a food.

"Oh, yes please," replied Odd, "any chance of any toast too?"

"Yes, OK. Are you sure I can't get you anything Svend?" she said turning to the much slimmer of the two visitors.

"No, no Jenny, I'm just fine with black coffee."

"Sam, do you want anything?"

"Er, what?" said Sam who was thinking about a million and one things, he hadn't even heard what she'd said.

"Breakfast?" said Jenny speaking a bit louder and slower.

"Breakfast?"

"Yeah, the thing you normally eat in the morning, kind of keeps up your strength for the rest of the day and all that!"

"Er, no thanks Jen, I'm alright," Sam turned to Svend, "so when do I go? To Norway I mean?"

"Oh, er, well normally we would have recommended a period of adjustment. You know you've had rather a big shock, first discovering you had parents and then finding out that they were killed. Normally it would be a few weeks or even a month maybe. Time for you to get used to the changes, space to think about the move, say goodbye to your friends, stuff like that."

"Say goodbye?" said Sam getting upset, "but Jenny and Spike, they'll be able to visit me, won't they?"

"Jenny and Spike? Sure, no problem, I'm sure we can arrange for them to fly over for school holidays, even for long weekends."

"Oh right, good."

"But the thing is Sam," started Svend cautiously, he paused, "that's what we would normally do, but in these circumstances I'm afraid that's not going to be possible."

"What do you mean "in these circumstances"?" asked Sam defensively.

Svend looked at Sarah who had been sat quietly listening to everything. Sarah was the person that Sam had known for the longest in the whole world. Although he never saw her as a mother figure, she did feel like an aunt or older sister. She'd always made sure that Sam was alright, he'd always been able to talk with her and she'd always been honest with him. Honesty was a big thing to Sam.

"Sarah! What does he mean?" asked Sam.

Sarah took a deep breath.

"Sam, when Odd and Svend called me early this morning they told me quite a few things about the crash."

"Right, like what?" Sam had a suspicious nature, maybe it was made worse by reading the books he did.

"About the accident," she continued.

Just at that moment Jenny walked into the room with slice of hot buttered toast in her hand, and couple of slices on a plate for Odd, on her way through from the kitchen she'd heard the conversation.

"They think it wasn't an accident Sam," she blurted out coldly.

"Not an accident?"

"Well," continued Jenny, "come on! Start piecing everything together Sam. How quickly they arrived after the crash. How they want to whisk you off to Norway straight away."

"I don't know what you're trying to say," said Sam.

"Think about it!" Jenny paused "Sam, your mum and dad didn't die in an accidental plane crash they were killed! Someone murdered them!"

Sam was reeling inside from the shock. He was kind of getting used to one shock after another, but this, this was something else.

"Murdered? You think they were murdered Jenny?"

"Yeah."

"Sarah, is this true?" asked Sam.

"Thanks Jenny," said Sarah sternly to Jenny, "we were trying to break it to him gently!"

"He deserves to know the truth Sarah," said an unrepentant Jenny .

"I know he does but there are ways and means!"

"I was just being straight with him, you know how much he likes honesty."

Sarah glared at Jenny, she never knew when to shut up.

Sam was sitting quietly. Now a million and one things were going through his head! Everything was starting to get on top of him. Getting too much. But he had to know everything.

He'd been kept in the dark about where he came from for years, but no more. He took a deep breath.

"So *were* they murdered?" he stared at Odd and Svend.

Svend paused for a second, he looked at Sarah and Odd, "Yes Sam, we think they were. All the evidence that we've discovered so far leads to this conclusion. We are not certain of course, there needs to be an investigation, but we think so."

"So, what does that mean for me then?"

"It means," said Jenny butting in again, "that whoever killed them might try and get to you next!"

8) 16 October 2011, 10.15 local time, Skreia, Norway, Freyer Becken's cottage.

82 year old Freyer Becken was pottering around her cosy wooden cottage in the small Norwegian village of Skreia in Oppland County, Norway. Freyer had no family, and to outsiders she would look like the classic old spinster. But to her friends in the close knit community she was everyone's favourite grandmother. She looked after everyone, she cooked for people when they were sick, cleaned their houses, chopped wood for their stoves. She looked after everyone's children and animals when needs be. Although in her eighties she had boundless energy. She was a pretty woman who when she'd been younger had been really beautiful. She had long white hair that she pulled and tied back. She always wore expensive, classy clothes. Her favourite colour was red. She always wore it, today she was wearing red trousers and a red woolly jumper.

But Freyer Becken had a secret. A secret that she had kept for over sixty years.

The television news was talking away in the background, Freyer liked the company. Suddenly she stopped what she was doing and stared at the screen, open mouthed.

"....who died tragically yesterday afternoon when their light aircraft crashed into a fjord, did have an heir after all. At the moment the details are sketchy but at our newsroom here in Oslo we have had an anonymous telephone call, which we will play for you now."

"Are you recording this call?" said a male voice in English.

"Yes Sir, all calls to the newsroom are recorded," replied the telephone operator at the newsroom.

"Good. Now make sure this tape gets played on air. You know the aircrash yesterday that everyone is going on about?"

"Yes, Sir."

"Everyone thought the Cheiftans were childless, right?"

"Yes Sir as far as I understood it they were."

"Well they weren't, there was a child, a boy."

"A boy?"

"Yeah, he lives in England, and even as we speak, Norwegian officials are speaking with him, they're going to bring him back to Norway, to be the new Chieftain..." the line went dead.

Freyer felt faint and sat down in her arm chair.

"That was a call made to us earlier today.." concluded the newsreader solemnly.

"My God?" said Freyer to herself, "He's alive, but he can't come home," suddenly she was talking to the television, "he's not safe here, not safe, how can he be? *He'll* find him. I know he will. I've got to get to him, tell him, help him!"

And with that Freyer rushed into her bedroom and started throwing clothes into a suitcase. She grabbed a long thick red coat and pulled on a pair of long black boots. Rushing out of her house she threw her suitcase onto the back seat of her old, but expensive BMW car. She sparked up the engine and zoomed off at breakneck speed out of the village, north west on her long journey to the islands.

9) 16 October 2011, 12.30 Leeds Airport, Yorkshire, England.

After hurriedly packing a couple of suitcases and saying a few brief, but sad, goodbyes Sam and Sarah had left with Svend and Odd in their black Mercedes and drove to Leeds Airport.

They had no idea that they were being followed by a grimy old van which always stayed two or three cars behind them. Whoever was driving knew exactly what they were doing.

At the airport entrance they were met by an airport security man who directed them to drive around the main terminal buildings and towards a military checkpoint around the side of the airfield. After their security passes were checked, the large metal gates were opened and they drove onto the air field and towards a private hangar well away from the other planes.

The van following them parked up and watched everything from a safe distance. They were not seen.

"Where are we going?" asked Sam a little confused.

Being at the airport was the only good thing that had happened to him in the past twelve hours or so. Sam Marsh loved planes. He loved the idea of flying. He and Spike would often catch a bus and come up to the airfield when a special plane or helicopter was due to arrive. They'd seen all sorts of aircraft here from an old World War 2 Lancaster Bomber to an immense Russian Antonov 124 transporter plane whose front end lifted right up allowing it to carry trucks and tanks. Sam and Spike were junior members of the local air club and so found out about everything that happened at the airport.

When Sam was really small, in fact just a toddler, Sarah had brought him up to see an Air France Concorde arrive in Yorkshire. Even though he was really young he clearly remembered how his chest and head had felt like they were going to explode when it landed! The vibration was fantastic and it made a sound like thunder, only this was thunder that went on and on! Sam remembered that there was a massive crowd of cheering people there to welcome the big white plane with swept back wings and a crooked nose. Everyone was so happy and friendly. It was the best day of his life. Concorde was so beautiful and sleek. Sam thought it was just perfect. When it took off the next day he wished he was flying it instead of watching from the airport cafe. On the day

Concorde flew for the last time Sam was almost in tears, it was the saddest day of his life, until today that is. But Sam vowed that one day he would be the pilot of a supersonic aircraft.

"Of course for security reasons we can't fly on a commercial plane," explained Odd, who had just started munching on a chocolate bar, "so instead we get to fly in our own jet."

"A private jet?" said Sam.

"Sure!"

Sam was thrown into a moment of complete panic.

"It's not a Cessna Citation is it?" he shouted, "It can't be a Cessna Citation!" Being an expert on planes Sam had remembered from the previous night's newsflash that the Cessna had been the plane that his parents had been flying home in the night before. Sam suddenly became really terrified.

"No, no, don't worry Sam," soothed Svend calmly, "it's not a Cessna Citation, I don't know much about planes, but I know that much!"

"Oh," Sam calming down instantly, "I suppose I'm just being stupid. I know it wasn't the plane's fault it crashed, I suppose a Cessna Citation is a really good plane."

"Yeah," agreed Odd, "it's a great plane."

"Sam, I think it's only natural that you're a little sensitive about what happened," said Sarah who had agreed to come along. Being an orphan was strange. You didn't have people for parents you had the council instead. They made all the decisions about your life, they decided where you lived and which school you went to. If you needed anything you had to ask them. It was weird but after all these years Sam had sort of got used to it.

But someone had to go with Sam to Norway, to be his guardian, and Sarah had known him longer than anyone else. She wasn't married and didn't have any children of her own so Sam had been pleased when she'd said she would go. Sarah had said it was the law that someone from the council went with him, and she said that she would stay with him until he became a proper Norwegian citizen. It was all very complicated and mind numbingly boring. But Sam was pleased that Sarah was going with him. Sarah hugged Sam.

"What are we going in then?" asked Sam, perking up at the thought of flying in a private jet. With a bit of luck he might even get to meet the pilots and look inside the cockpit whilst they were flying.

"Something very, very new and very, very fast," Odd was very excited at the thought, he'd told Sam that he loved planes too, but he was not clever enough to be a pilot and now he was far too fat. Svend had said that Odd couldn't even drive a car properly! He'd said he was a lunatic behind the wheel and that it was a really good thing that he was too stupid and fat to be a pilot! But Odd had flown in lots of planes and helicopters, from Harrier Jump Jets to Apache Attack helicopters. Sam was starting to see Odd in a different light, they had a lot in common and he was so funny.

They parked up just next to a closed hangar door and whilst they waited the doors slid slowly open.

"Wow!" said Sam and Odd together as they peered inside the hangar at the sharp pointy nose of a glistening new plane.

"Wow! I've never seen a plane like this before," said Sam "what is it?"

"Ask him," said Svend pulling a face and pointing to Odd, "he's the plane geek!"

"Yeah, I am Svend!" said Odd defiantly, "and I'm proud of it too!"

"Go on then Geek, tell him about it!" teased Svend shaking his head. Sometimes he felt he was the senior officer and Odd was the new kid on the block.

"Well Sam, I told you it was new. Very new."

"How new?" asked Sam walking around the plane, staring up in wonder, the plane was beautiful, like a small Concord.

"This is the first one!" said Odd proudly patting the bottom of the shiny swept back wings.

"But what is it? I don't recognise it."

"It's an Aerion SBJ!"

"Supersonic Business Jet?" asked Sam, his mouth gaping wide open, "Supersonic!" he said the word slowly.

"Yep, supersonic," replied Odd.

"SBJ! Awesome!" gawped Sam.

"Yeah it's well awesome!" agreed Odd.

"But I didn't think these things were on the market yet?"

"Well, I suppose they aren't, technically. Like I said this is the first one."

"But aren't these things really expensive? Like millions of dollars, expensive?"

"$80 million dollars expensive," said Odd proudly, "but we got ourselves the $80 million dollars and we got ourselves the first one!"

"Come on you two, let's get on board," said Svend getting bored with the plane geek talk!

"But this thing must fly at nearly Mach 2!" said Sam as he started climbing the stairs into the small, sleek, pointy white plane.

"Yeah nearly, officially it flies at Mach 1.8."

"Mach 1.8! Amazing. What's its ceiling?"

"He means, how high can it fly?" grinned Odd at Sarah. He then turned to Sam, "Fifty one thousand feet!" Odd knew all the facts off by heart.

"Wow! That's almost in space!" said Sam.

"Yep! Sure is, almost!"

"So how long will it actually take to get to the Lofoten Islands in this thing?" asked Sarah.

Sam and Odd were both rushing to work it out. It was a like a mini competition.

"About thirty minutes!" blurted out Sam, enthusiastically, after about ten seconds.

"Too quick Sam, you were too quick. You need to think about everything. You've got to remember take off and landing," said Odd grinning, "maybe forty five minutes with the wind behind her, but that was a fantastic guess Sam. Impressive, very impressive!"

"Not much wind that high up though, Odd."

"No, that's true, it's well above most of the weather systems."

Sam smiled, something he felt he hadn't done for ages. Just this time yesterday he was a normal boy who was sat in boring lessons with his friends. Now he had a flight in a brand new Aerion SBJ to look forward to and nothing could compare to that.

Svend shook his head, he leaned over to Sarah and whispered, chuckling, "I think there will be two little boys wanting to go up and meet the pilot!"

10) 16th October 2011, 13.50 Berlin local time, Exclusive top floor Kurfurstendamm apartment.

Herr Krater was sat at his desk speaking on the phone. He was a small skeleton like man whose skin was bleached white. He always wore black, black clothes, black hat, black glasses and he had a sinister air about him. He was old but no one knew how old. Krater was an ancient professor, highly intelligent, and he liked plans to fall neatly into place. Great importance was placed on doing thorough research and planning things down to the last detail. At first when he had discovered that the Chieftains of Lofoten had a child he was angry. He had not been fully informed and this had upset his plan. But after giving the matter careful thought he decided that the best solution to the problem created by young Sam Marsh was his immediate elimination. This was Krater's usual answer to something he didn't like, get rid of it.

As long as Sam Marsh was alive then there would be someone with power, influence and birthright to stop The Company, even though the boy was only 12 years old. Cost was not important to Krater, he had almost a trillion dollars secretly stowed in various banks around the planet. He also had assets, he owned shares in almost every large company in the world, he was a major player in the arms business and had secretly stashed many of the weapons his companies had developed over the decades. He also owned a lot of property, hundreds of thousands of properties. He'd amassed his vast empire over sixty long years. When he'd started they tried to take what he had, take everything and give it back to those people, the liars. But no one had succeeded and he'd got more and more powerful as the years passed. But he always remained in the shadows, he was almost a shadow himself. Officially he'd died in 1952 as the result of a car accident. But he hadn't, he planned the stunt personally and was delighted when everything went like clockwork.

What was important, though, always, was success and the child was a minor obstacle in his way. Sam Marsh would be eliminated as he flew to Norway, there would be no evidence, no survivors, the matter would be resolved quickly, clinically. Herr Krater did not tolerate failure.

"They are boarding the private jet, Herr Krater, Sir." said the man on the line in Russian.

"When are they due to depart?" asked Krater, he knew that for the procedure he was planning that perfect timing was crucial.

"Very soon Sir, maybe 13.00 hours local time, conditions permitting, I am logged into the airport computer system and they are cleared to go in the next departure slot, they are just awaiting a commercial arrival from Spain."

"You have been most professional, Chigashev, I will not forget this. I will require you and Frolov in Norway, I have work for you. Thank you."

Krater didn't wait for a response, he didn't do pleasantries, he didn't have time, he just put the phone down and immediately logged on to his computer. An instant video link came on screen. There was a man waiting for orders.

"Herr Krater, what are my orders, Sir?"

"There is a private jet leaving Leeds Airport within the next ten minutes, destination Svolvaer, The Lofoten Islands, Norway, Belloch's orders are to intercept and destroy it."

"Sir!"

"There is to be no evidence. It is to be obliterated, do you understand what I'm saying?"

"Yes sir, we use the Genie."

"Yes, the Genie."

11) 16 October 2011, 1pm Leeds Airport.

"Ok, everyone," said Anita, one of the stewardesses, "Er, excuse me! If you two could stop chattering," she stared at Sam and Odd who were like two excited school boys, "and watch Hilde for a few moments, she's going to demonstrate the emergency procedures for this aircraft. I'm afraid even vip planes have to follow rules!"

After Hilde had demonstrated how to pull on a royal life jacket and blow a royal whistle, everyone strapped themselves in for take-off from the Yorkshire airport.

When the engines fired up the rumble was awesome.

"Wow it sounds just like Concord!" said Sam.

"Did you fly on her Sam?" asked Odd.

"Me? No, but I saw her come here, did you?"

"Yep," said Odd proudly, "I saved up.."

"And emptied your piggy bank!" butted in Svend chuckling.

"I saved up and went to New York. I could only afford to fly on her one way so I had to take the slow plane back."

The Aerion started moving slowly as its engines rumbled gently. Suddenly it set off, the force pinning everyone in to their seats. It sped powerfully towards the end of the long runway and took off, soaring smoothly above the rain soaked Yorkshire countryside. Sam craned his neck to peer out of the window as it banked sharply. Far below was Ilkley Moor where Jessie had sometimes taken them and the dogs for walks, when she could still walk and when there was no bingo on the telly. In the distance he thought he could see Malham Cove, in the Yorkshire Dales where he'd visited once with school. He'd been fascinated to discover that it had once been a waterfall even bigger and more powerful than Niagara Falls! He loved the idea that Niagara Falls had once been in Yorkshire. He was proud to be a Yorkshire person, or at least he had thought he was a Yorkshire person until this morning.

Suddenly the chatter in the cabin was broken by the voice of the captain over the loudspeakers.

"God dag!" he said in Norwegian, "This is Captain Harket speaking to you this morning. Welcome to our plane! Hello Sam, you are our special guest on this royal flight to Svolvaer in the Lofoten Islands. Today, it will take us about one hour, which is longer than you would expect for this plane. There is a head wind. It is a strong north easterly wind which is blowing right in our face. That's why we call it a headwind!"

"He thinks we're stupid!" whispered Odd to Sam who sniggered.

"You are stupid!" added Svend.

Captain Harket continued unawares, "...this will affect the low level parts of the flight. That will slow this bullet plane up a little I'm afraid, but we will still be flying supersonic and todays flight ceiling will be 49 thousand feet, almost in space! And now for Sam. In a little while, when we've left UK airspace, you will be able to come up to the cockpit and help us fly the plane Sam, if you like!"

Sam gasped excitedly," If I like?"

"I wonder if I can come up too?" said Odd.

"I'll ask Captain Harket, Odd, but I can't promise anything!" teased Sam.

"Just a little more information for you. I think we should have a smooth flight today. Flying conditions are quite good. The weather in Svolvaer is a chilly 6 degrees, and it's drizzling a little."

"Like Yorkshire!" joked Sarah.

"Just like Yorkshire!" repeated the Captain comically just as if he could hear her.

"He likes the sound of his own voice." whispered Odd.

"...It will be early afternoon when we arrive, but because Svolvaer is in the Arctic Circle, it will be starting to get dark. That is all from me for now. Please enjoy your journey. Anita and Hilde will be serving hot chocolate, coffee, sandwiches, waffles and cakes in a little while. Oh, and yes, we know Sam, you're a vegetarian, so just for you, because you're the new Chieftain, everyone will be eating vegetarian food for lunch. Thank you."

Sam grinned, perhaps this being Chieftain business wasn't so bad after all? He could order everyone to be vegetarian!

12) 16 October 2011, 13.05. Outside Leeds Airport.

Chigashev and Frolov emptied the surveillance equipment from the battered old van into a black Range Rover which had blackened windows. The two immense men looked like massive weightlifters and stood out from the other people around the airport. They had close cropped, soldier's hair and were wearing black leather jacket. On their feet were lace up boots giving away, to the more observant, that they were soldiers. But to the untrained eye they looked more like mean cyborgs than people. They worked like robots in complete silence.

As they were emptying the van a security patrol car pulled up alongside them. The fat guard in a dark blue uniform got out and made his way towards the men, he was munching on a bag of crisps. The two Russians ignored the man and continued their work.

"Er hum!" the guard cleared his throat, normally people took notice of him, nobody ever wanted a parking ticket or their wheels clamping! He usually got respect from people.

Jonathan Milner had been a security patrol man at Leeds Airport for five years. The pay wasn't too great but everyone treated you with respect. Everyone looked up to you. Sometimes they even called you 'sir'! As a security patrol no day was ever the same and Jonathan always looked forward to going to work. Sure, sometimes people got angry with him, sometimes they shouted or called him rude names, but he'd been taught from day one that he must never back down or show any weakness. He'd developed a thick skin.

"Excuse me gents," said Jonathan puffing his chest out proudly.

There was no response and the men continued to ignore him.

"Excuse me gents, I'm afraid you can't park here, it's a restricted area. No parking at any time. Can't you read the signs?" he pointed to a sign that was right next to the Range Rover.

The big Russians continued to ignore the man and continued their work in complete silence. It was just like Jonathan Milner didn't exist.

"Gentlemen, didn't you hear me, I said, you can't park here!" said the guard a little louder, he was getting annoyed, they were going to get a ticket, or he might even call the clamping squad.

He walked towards the men, looking curiously over their shoulders in their van.

"Hey! What are you two doing, what's in that van? What're you moving?"

Still no answer.

The guard stepped back and turned his back on the men, he started speaking into his radio, "Security patrol 271, look, I think I might have a problem.."

Thud! Frolov threw the guard into the side of their van winding him badly. Quickly Chigashev grabbed a roll of duct tape and roughly stuck a huge piece of it over the guard's mouth. Frolov smashed Milner into the van again and he crumbled to the floor, knocked out cold. Chigashev taped up his wrists and ankles and they bundled him back into his car, turned off the engine, pulled out the keys and threw them away.

"Is no problem, thank you very much!" Chigashev grinned at his colleague in broken English.

"No problem!" replied Frolov grinning.

Chigashev released the handbrake and grabbed the steering wheel and started pushing the van onto the grass. Frolov went behind the van and pushed his shoulder up to the back door. The men slowly moved the van forward and along the verge. They pushed quicker and quicker and suddenly they were running. It was like they were back in the toboggan. They reached the edge of the grassy bank and jumped free watching the van career down the slope into the fence where it came to a halt.

The men quickly returned to their work. Once the van was completely empty, Frolov took a can of petrol and doused it with the smelly liquid, he backed off a little and then he threw in a lit match. He moved quickly then, really quickly for such a big man and dived into the Range Rover as it sped off out of the airport.

13) 16 October 2011, 1327, High over the North Sea.

After piles of cheese and veggie-ham sandwiches, vegetarian sausages, cakes, delicious waffles and hot chocolate had been enjoyed by everyone, especially Odd, Sam had been allowed to meet Captain Harket and Co-Pilot Nilsen in the cockpit. He'd even been allowed to fly the plane for a while. Odd had been allowed into the cockpit but not allowed to fly the plane.

"I'm afraid you're not a vip guest, Mr Aukland," said Nilsen apologetically.

"I'm sorry Odd, Svend tells me that you're a terrible driver!" joked Captain Harket.

"But Sam's just a boy, and you allowed him to fly it," sulked Odd.

"He might be just a boy, Odd," grinned Nilsen, "but haven't you forgotten something?"

"What?"

"He also happens to be the new Chieftain of Lofoten!" the two pilots roared with laughter as Odd skulked back to the others.

The plane was amazing, the controls were so responsive. Just the smallest of touches on the controls made the plane move such a long way. And Sam was really impressed that the cockpit looked like the inside of a space ship.

Rejoining the others in the comfort of the lounge area, Sam had decided when he grew up he would definitely become a pilot. It must be fantastic to fly such a fast and beautiful plane as this. But maybe he would learn to fly in the air force, that way he could fly war planes too!

Just as Sam was sitting back down in his chair, red warning lights started flashing all around the lounge.

"What's going on?" shouted Sarah.

"Sit down everyone!" shouted Svend, "something's wrong!"

"Fasten your seat belts," called Anita, who was rushing back to her place at the back of the plane, checking all the passengers were buckled up, "quickly Sam, fasten your seatbelt, you too Odd, OK, everyone done? Good."

"I reckon we're being tracked," shouted Odd.

"Tracked?" replied Sarah, "what does that mean?"

"A missile!" shouted Sam confidently, "we're being tracked by a computer controlled pre-programmed missile!"

"Tracked by a missile?" shouted Sarah panicking, "someone's fired a missile at us?"

"Don't listen to them Sarah, they don't know, it might just be something more normal," said Svend.

"This isn't normal Svend!" cried Odd.

"Calm down everyone," said Sam, "and let Captain Harket deal with it, he's a great pilot you know," Sam was desperately trying to believe his own words, though he knew enough about this kind of weapon to know that once it had locked on to its target it was almost certainly going to hit! And then they would be blown into a million pieces!

Suddenly the plane jerked violently to the left, then to the right, then left, then right. Then it started to dive headlong towards the sea, down and down it dropped like a lead weight. Captain Harket sent the plane rocking violently from one side to another as the plane nose dived but this time at a phenomenal speed.

"He's trying to avoid it!" called out Sam excitedly.

"Yeah, it's the only way we'll survive. He is a great pilot!" agreed Odd.

Sam craned his neck to peer out of his window, he couldn't see the missile anywhere but he knew it must be there. Then he saw it. He knew instantly what it was, but things didn't make sense.

"It's a Genie!" he called out.

"A Genie?" said Sarah.

"It can't be Sam, you must be wrong, they haven't been about for years."

"It's a Genie Odd, I'd know one anywhere."

"What's a Genie?" asked Sarah in a panic.

"A Genie, Sarah, is an air to air rocket that carries a warhead," explained Odd.

"A warhead?" now Svend was worried.

"Yeah a nuclear warhead," said Sam calmly.

"But the AIR-2 Genies weren't guided missiles Sam," said Odd.

"Well this one is."

Sam was still peering out of the window when suddenly a plane came hurtling towards them and shot past them, Sam recognised it immediately as an F15, swing wing jet fighter, but he didn't know which airforce it belonged to as he wasn't quick enough to see the tail markings. A couple of seconds later another F15 thundered past in the same direction!

The passengers were all thrown backwards in their seats as Captain Harket pulled the passenger jet into a viciously steep climb. Sam felt his whole body get heavy, really heavy, he felt like he was being pinned to his seat, he couldn't even move his arms, it was like they were tied down with invisible rope. They were climbing towards the edge of space! This must be how astronauts feel when they blast off, thought Sam.

Less than three seconds later there was an immensely loud explosion below them which rocked the plane hard. Gradually, after the explosion subsided, they began to level off and slow down a little.

There was complete silence in the passenger lounge as everyone tried to regain their composure. Sarah had turned as white as a sheet.

"Ladies and gentlemen," a familiar, calm voice came over the loudspeakers, "this is Captain Harket here, I must apologise for throwing you all about so much, I don't normally do this to my passengers, especially important ones," he seemed very jolly considering the events of the last few minutes.

Sam grinned, the whole event was so exciting, he was getting to like this being a somebody business.

"..but we have just been attacked by an enemy missile, the origin of which is for the moment unknown. Thankfully, just as I was taking evasive action two colleagues from the airforce, who had been tracking us, flew close by and were able to destroy the missile. I can assure you that they have called for further reinforcements and in the meantime will continue to accompany us onwards to our destination of Svolvaer. I do hope there will be no further incidents."

When Sam looked around he could see Sarah and Svend sat very upright in their chairs gripping the arm rests hard and looking very uncomfortable. Looking over to Odd, he was excitedly peering out of the window looking for the F15's, just as Sam had done a few seconds earlier.

"I think it was fired from a sub!" he declared to Sam.

"Maybe," replied Sam, "but I don't know Odd, it's so hard to tell you know, but I have a feeling it might have been fired from another plane, it was an air to air missile after all. If it had have been from a sub I think it would have hit us."

"Is everyone alright?" said Anita walking up the aisle looking a little stunned, but still smart in her red uniform.

"Can we get anyone anything?" asked Hilde following.

"I am feeling a little faint Hilde, maybe a piece of cake or a biscuit might help?" said Odd.

"Odd!" said Svend slowly.

"Odd what?"

"You're always thinking of your belly!"

"Well, we all need a little sugar boost, we've just had a big shock you know!"

"Can I have a ticket back to Yorkshire!" said Sarah half jokingly.

"That was great!" said Sam who had thoroughly enjoyed the whole incident.

"That was a close thing," said Svend, "I think we are going to have to think long and hard about your safety, Sam Marsh."

"But I'm the Chieftain of Lofoten, I'm just going home, nothing can stop that," said Sam quietly.

14) 16 October 2011, 13.41pm, The North Sea

As the unmarked Harrier jump jet landed heavily on the specially made deck of the small fishing trawler, Belloch quickly unhooked his safety belts and pushed up the visor of his helmet. Two men had appeared from the cabin with ladders and had climbed up and lifted up the glass hood of the plane.

"Krater wants to speak with you on the video link," said one of the men in a heavy Russian accent.

"Great!" said Belloch sarcastically as he clambered out, Herr Krater made him feel very nervous. He made him feel that something nasty was going to happen at any moment. He'd heard terrible stories about him. Belloch was starting to wish he'd never agreed to work for The Company. Sure, the money was fantastic but he had a bad feeling about his employer. Herr Krater was such a creepy guy.

As soon as Belloch had climbed out of the Harrier the two men closed the hatch and heaved a huge smelly old tarpaulin up and over the jet. The men pulled and manoeuvred a boon to directly above the jump jet and suddenly piles and piles of smelly fish and ice were dumped over the plane, completely covering it.

"No one will ever know it's here Misha!" grinned the older of the two men to the other in Russian. The sight of his disgusting brown teeth made the other feel sick again. Misha couldn't help it, those teeth were rancid!

As Belloch made his way through the cramped fishing ship, he took off his helmet and gloves. Ducking through the low hatch as he entered the bridge he saw the large computer screen on which was the view of the back of Krater's leather chair facing out over a city's roof tops. He didn't recognise the view.

He cleared his throat, "Er hum! You wanted to speak to me, Sir?"

There was no response from the man who seemed to be in a trance as he stared across the city, Belloch couldn't be sure where it was. Not London or Paris, he knew that much but he couldn't be sure where. Maybe Krater was dead, that would be a stroke of good luck! That would solve all Belloch's problems if he had died just sitting in his chair waiting to talk with him! He crossed his fingers.

"Sir? Sir?"

"I heard you the first time, Belloch!" spat out the calm, rasping voice of Krater, he was obviously very angry.

"I fired the Genie Sir."

"Your missile missed!" came the hushed voice, "how can a pilot fire a pre-programmed missile, a state of the art missile that costs millions of dollars, which once fired, homes in on its target. How can this missile miss its target? It cannot miss Belloch! So how did it?"

"But the passenger jet was faster than I expected," blurted out Belloch, "I've never seen anything like it before, it must have been flying at Mach 2, way too fast for me! Those Harriers aren't fast planes you know!"

"It's fast enough, Belloch!" shouted Krater.

"And another thing," argued Belloch pathetically, "those F15's! They came out of nowhere, they shot at me, I had no choice, I had only one clear shot at the passenger jet! I couldn't get the second Genie away! And they're heavy missiles you know, really too heavy for a Harrier!"

"The Harrier was specially adapted!"

"Well I got one away!"

"And that one shot was a bad one!" Krater was furious.

"I still fired!"

"You were given precise information Belloch, you were given a Harrier Jump jet, a perfect vantage point and two specially built AIR-2 Genie, nuclear tipped rockets that have heat-seeking capabilities and you still missed!"

"Sir, I will succeed next time, I swear. I give you my word. I eradicated the old Chieftains last night didn't I?"

"I am a patient man," said Krater quietly, "and I grant you that one success. You did eradicate the others, but you failed to disable the black box in the process! And you were the captain!"

"What?"

"Last night that plane should have been vaporised when it hit the fjord, your explosive device must not have detonated! You must have set it wrong.."

"I set it perfectly."

Krater continued, "..and that plane today should have been vaporised by that 10 million dollar Genie rocket, a weapon so advanced that no-one in the world has access to it except us. There should have been not one single shred of evidence of either incident!"

"But it's impossible to do that!" argued Belloch, "there's always some evidence in an air crash!"

"You should know me by now, Captain Belloch, I expect the impossible!" shouted Krater who still hadn't turned around. "The black box will allow them to find out what happened you fool!"

"But.."

"No buts Belloch, two failures and our agreement is at an end, finished!"

"What? Agreement at an end? But you can't do that, I've got a contract!"

"You'll find I can and you'll find your contract is worthless! Our agreement is terminated Mr Belloch forthwith!"

"Well if that's what you want," said Belloch warily, "just give me my two million dollars then I will be on my way."

"Very well Captain. It is there on the desk behind you. You might like to count it first."

"Naw, that's alright, I trust you," Belloch had a feeling he ought to get off the ship as soon as possible. He didn't trust Krater one little bit!

"Never trust anyone," advised Krater wisely, "that's my last piece of advice to you Captain."

Slowly Belloch turned around and, sure enough, there was a black briefcase on the desk behind him. He walked cautiously to the desk watching for the appearance of an armed attacker or something. He wouldn't put anything passed Krater. He flipped the case open. Inside were two million dollars in toy Monopoly money!

"What is this?" he shouted, "You've cheated me!"

"You don't understand do you Belloch? It's all one big game. One big, big game Captain, and, guess what?"

"What?"

"I'm the banker."

"Banker?"

"These are my instructions to you, Captain." Krater spoke slowly and firmly, enjoying the moment, "Go directly to jail, do not pass go, do not collect two million dollars," Krater was laughing as he pressed the big red button firmly that was on the arm of his chair hundreds of miles away in Berlin.

Suddenly the floor beneath Belloch's feet dropped away. For a split second Belloch was stood in thin air, staring down in disbelief like a bizarre cartoon character, then suddenly he dropped into the icy sea below.

From his office Krater was roaring with evil laughter.

"Have a nice swim, it's only seventy five miles to the shore, if you can survive the freezing water that is!"

Krater loved his own sick jokes!

15) Saturday 16th October 2011, 15.30 local time, Svolvaer, The Lofoten Islands, Norway.

Svolvaer Airport was tiny compared to Leeds. Just one small runway and no big jets anywhere. Instead there were mainly small planes and helicopters dotted around the sides of the runway. As the Aerion plane came to a rolling stop Captain Harket came on the loudspeaker for a final time.

"Landed safely, I hope our little problem didn't upset anyone too much. I do apologise for it and hope, Your Chieftan-ness, that you will settle into your new home in Norway. Norway welcomes you!"

Anita opened the door and a gust of damp wind blew into the small plane.

"I thought it snowed in Norway?" said Sam a little disappointed.

"It does Sam, and you will get plenty of snow to play in," answered the Stewardess, "but it's still early autumn you know, and the Lofoten Islands being so close to the sea do get less snow than other parts of Norway."

"And it's because it's close to the Gulf Stream!" said Sam.

"Sam!" called Sarah as Sam got set to step out, "coat on please!" ordered Sarah trying to put the coat onto Sam's excited flapping arms.

As Sam pulled his new puffa coat on, a large man walked towards the plane. The man was even fatter than Odd, with white hair and a white beard and a big grin on his face. In fact he looked a lot like Santa, only the fact that he wasn't wearing a red suit made Sam doubt it actually was Santa.

Sam gawped at the man as he walked up the steps. He had a magical kind of look about him.

"Is this Santa?" whispered Sam out of the corner of his mouth trying not to be overheard by the man.

"Ha, ha! I do look a bit like Santa, Sam, but I'm afraid I'm not him, a lot of Norwegians up here look like him because you know, Santa, he is a Norwegian! Did you know that Sam?"

"No, I always thought he came from Lapland?" said Sam.

"Well, Lapland is a part of Norway, Sam, and I can assure you that Santa is from the Norwegian part, not the Swedish one! Nobody must ever think that Santa is from Sweden or worse Finland! He is Norwegian!"

"Oh! So he's not from Sweden or Finland?" Sam was trying to get it right in his head.

"No, no, Santa is not Swedish or heaven forbid, Finnish, now that would be terrible! A Finnish Santa Claus! Whatever next?"

"Oh!" said a subdued Sam.

"Actually Santa has quite a quiet time up here in Norway."

"He does?"

"Ja, for sure, in Norway all the presents are delivered by Julenissen, they are Christmas elves and they do all the work for Santa."

"They do!"

"Ja they do. Anyway I'll tell you all about Julenissen later. Greetings! I am very pleased to meet you Sam," The man stuck out a podgy hand," My name is Hammer, and before you say anything, it might sound a bit funny in English but here in Norway it's a real name for sure. I promise."

"Nice to meet you Hammer," said Sam shaking his hand, he was getting used to meeting lots of strange people.

"I'm your, how do you say in English? The Mayor."

"You're the Mayor of Svolvaer?" asked Sam.

"Ja! I am. I'm the Mayor and I am going to make sure that you settle in here in the Lofoten Islands."

"But what about Odd and Svend?" asked a worried Sam, he had grown to like them, especially Odd, who felt like the uncle he had never had.

"Oh, they will still be around all the time,"

"Can't get rid of us that easily Sam," joked Odd.

"Ja," explained Hammer, "Svend and Odd are in charge of keeping you safe and sound. I'm in charge of making sure that you have everything you need. I look after your household, your education, your public duties."

"Do I have to do public duties?" asked Sam.

"Ja, sure, not straight away, but you're like the new crown prince here and after you have settled in there will be lots of things you will have to do around all the islands. But first you must settle in, then you will get to meet all the people that live here in Lofoten."

"That sounds like a lot of work," said Sam, slightly daunted.

"Oh don't worry Sam, you'll get used to your duties. And it won't take up all your time, apart from school time there will be lots of time for playing games, exploring, meeting other kids. Don't worry. Lofoten is a great place to live!"

"I'm actually an inventor," said Sam.

"An inventor?" asked Hammer.

"Yeah."

"Then I'll make sure you have a workshop where you can invent things!"

The group got off the plane and got into a large black Range Rover, Hammer was driving this time. As they drove out of the airport, Sam had his first taste of Norway. It was nearly dark and all the brightly coloured wooden houses were awash with light. Every single light in Lofoten seemed to be on at the same time. It looked magical, even though it was drizzling.

"Wow! It's so beautiful, has everyone got their lights on?" asked Sarah.

"Oh that's normal in Norway," explained Hammer, "everyone loves light, and nobody ever draws their curtains up here. I think it must be because we have such long, dark nights in winter. Do you know Sam that for a whole month at the end of the year there is hardly any daylight at all."

"Really? Is it night all day?"

"Well not exactly pitch black, it's just kind of dusky for most of the day, and then it gets dark in the early afternoon."

"Well, I don't know about darkness but the roads are really very quiet," said Sarah as they drove along, "it's a bit different from Leeds on a Saturday afternoon."

"Oh, it's quieter than England then?" asked Hammer.

"Yeah, much, much quieter than England."

"I've been to visit London and it was very loud," said Hammer.

"It might be quieter and while Norway might not have that many cars on its roads its drivers certainly like to make up for it," said Svend giving Odd a hard look.

"I'll have you know Sam, I'm a great driver," said Odd, "I could have been a racing car driver you know?"

"What stopped you?" asked Sam.

"He kept on crashing!" interrupted Svend, nudging Odd and laughing.

"Yeah, everyone drives pretty crazy in Norway," continued Hammer.

"Why's that then, Hammer?" asked Sarah.

"Oh, Svend and Odd are not so wrong, it's because everyone, like Odd here, thinks they're a formula one driver! They're crazy! And some of the roads on the islands are pretty, how do you say, hairy?"

"Oh heck!" said Sarah gulping.

"Oh look everyone, we are nearly at your new home."

The Range Rovers pulled off the main road that ran out of Svolvaer and onto a short driveway that was blocked by large iron gates. There were a couple of guards at the gate who approached the car. The soldiers had guns in their hands and looked fierce. But when they saw it was the grinning Hammer at the wheel they just smiled and waved them through the automatic gates. They were even pulling silly faces at Sam as they drove through. Sam returned the faces by stretching his mouth wide and thrusting his tongue at them. The guards laughed as they closed the gates.

16) 16 October 2011, 16.00, Helipad on top of exclusive Kurfurstendamm apartment.

Herr Krater walked with a stick towards the idling black Bell 206 Jet Ranger helicopter. As well as having black paintwork all the windows were blackened, it bore just one letter on it sides, a large gold "C".

Slowly the old man made his way to the open door. Herr Krater always refused assistance of any kind, although extremely old he still had the view that to need assistance was a sign of weakness and Krater did not accept weakness, from others always, but from himself, never!

Tonight he would fly to Neuwerk a small island off the north sea coast of Germany where he would rendezvous with his private X boat which would take him north to the scene of his treasure. It would also take him closer to the person who was becoming his young nemesis, Sam Marsh.

17) 16 October 2011, 17.00 The Royal Villa, Svolvaer. Settling in.

Sam was enjoying settling into the plush 'Royal Villa', that was the locals nickname for Sam's new home. It was certainly better than living on a council estate in Holmford. Apart from the fuss that everyone made of him, the villa was fantastic. It was massive with easily fifteen bedrooms. But inside everything was wooden, wooden walls, wooden floors, comfortable chairs and sofas. And his bed room was enormous. Bigger than his classroom back at school and much more comfy. It had a big double bed in the middle, its own TV that showed English satellite telly. It even showed a TV channel that showed programmes about inventors and inventions all day long. Sam planned to stay up all night watching it. But best of all there was a brand new laptop on a desk. He even had his own bathroom and toilet. The villa didn't seem like any palaces he's seen in books or on TV, and it was nothing like Buckingham Palace, it was more like a big, fantastic, comfy cabin.

Sam ran downstairs and found everyone sat around a big table in the huge kitchen. The housekeeper, Jorunn, was busy. She was a big plump lady with white hair and bright red cheeks. She had made loads of cakes and buns, and there was a funny red can on the table for him.

"What's this?" asked Sam inspecting the can cautiously, he didn't know what it was.

"It's a drink for you Sam," said Jorunn.

"But what is it?"

"It's Solo," she replied

"What's Solo? I've never heard of it!"

"It's a drink you get in Norway. It's very popular."

"But what does it taste like, Jorunn?"

"Well Sam, there's only one way to find out," she laughed, "if you open it you'll find out what it tastes like."

Sam carefully opened the ring pull, opened the can and took a small sip.

"Taste's a bit like fizzy orange," he declared. He looked over and saw that Odd was drinking a can a bit like his, "Do you like it too, Odd?"

"He likes it Sam but he has to have Solo Lett!" laughed Svend drinking coffee.

"I don't *have* to have Solo Lett, Svend, but it's just happens that I like the taste better," argued Odd.

"You do not Odd, and we both know that they taste exactly the same."

"What's Solo Lett?" asked Sam.

"It's the same as Solo, Sam," answered Jorunn, "but it's got less sugar in it, it's for.."

"Fat people like Odd!" said Svend laughing.

"Yeah, yeah!" said Odd sipping his Solo Lett.

"Sam," said Hammer sipping a coffee, "Jorunn has made a special cake to celebrate your arrival in Norway."

"A special cake?" said Sam.

"Ja, it's a special cake that Norwegians have when they are celebrating something good and your arrival is very good."

"Is it?" said Sam, not quite understanding how important he'd become.

"Ja, for sure Sam," said Jorunn, "when we heard about the crash and the death of our most loved ones we were so sad, it was a terrible shock, but then we discovered that they had a son, and that you were coming back to Lofoten to live, it made everyone feel so happy. Still a little sad about the crash but happy that you were alive. It was a very good surprise."

"It was a surprise for me too," nodded Sam.

"Ja, we know, but we will all get some answers when there is an investigation," said Hammer.

"When is the investigation?" asked Sam, he was keen to know about the death of his mum and dad.

"It has started this morning already, Sam. They have to look for.." Hammer paused and looked at Sarah.

"They have to look for bodies Sam," said Sarah gently.

"Yeah, I know that," said Sam, "I'm not a kid you know."

"No, I know you're not Sam, but it's not very nice for anyone when someone close to them dies."

"I wasn't close to them," said Sam staring into his can, "I didn't know them, they abandoned me."

Jorunn rushed around the table, picked Sam up and gave him a big hug. No one had ever hugged Sam properly. Jessie never hugged him and he never wanted her to anyway. This was a really strange feeling for Sam, but it somehow felt nice. After a couple of minutes Jorunn put Sam back down and she shuffled back to the stove. A few seconds later she turned around. In her arms was the biggest, tallest cake you could imagine. It was massive. Like a big pyramid cake, that was easily half a metre high. It was drizzled with white icing and had loads of little Norwegian and British flags stuck into it.

"Wow!" said Sam.

"Wow!" agreed Odd, licking his lips.

"This is the special cake Sam," said Hammer, "it's called a Kransekake."

"What does Kransekake mean?" asked Sam.

"It means ring cake," explained Jorunn, "you see, if you look you can see that it's made up of lots of ring cakes put on top of each other, the ring cake at the bottom is big and the one at the top is the smallest."

"Wow, it's excellent!" gasped Sam, "can I have a piece?"

"For sure!" said Jorunn placing it on the table and fetching a large, sharp knife. She cut Sam a huge piece and then cut pieces for everyone else.

"Can I just have a small piece please Jorunn?" asked Sarah.

"Can I have a big piece?" asked Odd.

"It's delicious!" said Sam, as he bit into the cake. It tasted of sweet almonds.

After they'd finished their tea, Hammer got up from the table.

"I've got a surprise for you Sam," he said.

"A surprise?" said Sam a little worried.

"Don't worry it's a good one, follow me."

Sam followed Hammer out of the kitchen, and out of the back door of the house. It was dark so he put some lights on and led the way towards a large wooden barn. He opened the door and put the lights on.

"Come in, come in Sam."

Inside it was amazing, it was a big workshop. There were loads of tools stuck up on the walls, tools for making things out of wood and metal. One side of the workshop looked like a laboratory and had lots of strange looking gadgets and gizmos.

"Wowee!" said Sam, open mouthed.

"You like it?"

"Like it? I love it! It's what I've always dreamed of! Somewhere where I can invent things, and these tools."

"Oh yes Sam, about the tools," said Hammer cautiously, "you must remember that you are still only young and some of these tools can be very dangerous."

"I know, I know!" Sam was so excited.

"You must promise me.."

"I promise, I promise, anything!"

"Sam, listen to me!" Hammer was firm.

"OK," Sam was listening.

"You must promise me that you ask an adult when you want to use these tools, promise!"

"I promise," said Sam running off to explore everything in his workshop, "Hammer?"

"Ja."

"Is it OK if I bring my computer into my workshop, it will help me invent things."

"Ja, sure."

18) 16 October 2011, 17.30 Neuwerk, boarding the X boat.

One mile off the small coastal village of Neuwerk on the German North Sea coast sat a large square pontoon. A floating platform it was anchored to the deep sea bed. At each corner was a red flashing light. Signalling its position to anyone arriving from the air. Suddenly from the west a Helicopter came into view. It was approaching quickly. It circled around the pontoon slowly and came in to land. It hovered and slowly came down to the platform, landing gently. No one got out as the helicopter's engines slowed down and stopped.

Suddenly, the waves next to pontoon started to part. Rising up from the sea came a huge tower, a huge long, thin black fin rose up higher and higher out of the murky depths. Then followed the rest of the monstrous submarine, which at 225 metres long was easily the biggest submarine ever built. Bigger even than the Seawolf Class submarines that the United States Navy commissioned in the 1980's and 1990's. Whilst the United States cancelled their orders for the mega subs after completing just three boats, The Company had taken the design of large nuclear powered submarines to a new level. So far they had built 25 of these vast weapons at a total cost of more than $40 billion.

Unlike conventional submarines these X boat class submarines ran on a minimal human crew being able to utilise The Company's advancements in a cybernetic organism development. On board was a skeleton human crew of fifteen alongside 50 cyborgs.

X boat 1A was Herr Krater's personal submarine and it would take him secretly on the long journey to the Norwegian Lofoten Islands high in the Arctic Circle. As a hatch opened at the base of the tall fin four silver humanoid figures emerged from the X boat and heaved a boarding ramp across to the pontoon. The captain of the sub emerged from the fin and walked down off the sub and onto the pontoon. Herr Krater emerged from the helicopter and was met by Commander Herman Bader.

Herman Bader wore a smart navy coloured uniform and cap, a tall bearded, upright man he held his hand out to shake Krater's.

"Herr Krater, we are ready for our mission."

"Thank you Commander Bader, how long do you anticipate the journey will take?" Krater was in a hurry to get to his Unterwasserwelt, his massive mobile underwater city that was making its way slowly to the Lofoten Islands.

"Herr Krater, we are the fastest submarine ever built Sir, we can easily make sixty knots, but the Unterwasserwelt has a top speed of only 15 knots, she will not be in position for three days, I suggest we proceed slowly, using the time to finalise our plans."

"What do you suggest?"

"I suggest, Sir, that we make a rendezvous in three days time."

"But you don't understand, I need to get to Lofoten quickly Bader," snapped Krater.

"Sir, I suggest that it would be best if we don't get to our destination too soon, it is not good to be waiting around. We might arouse some suspicion, we may be spotted. We do not want our plans to become known at this crucial point." Bader was an experienced submariner, he always thought things through very carefully.

"Very well Commander," agreed Krater, "we will proceed slowly for a rendezvous in three days time."

Krater walked passed Bader and up the gangway onto his X boat 1A, as he walked passed the robots they all bowed their heads in respect for their creator. Krater stopped and turned to Bader.

"Remind me Bader, how many X-boats have we built so far?"

"Number twenty six will be completed in two weeks time Herr Krater," replied Commander Bader proudly.

"Excellent news," said Krater walking in to the fin of the X boat.

Bader followed Krater and the humanoids dismantled the ramp as the helicopter took off and headed back to land.

Within two minutes X boat 1A had moved away from the pontoon and glided out to sea, quickly it started disappearing beneath the dark waves and into the depths of the North Sea.

19) 16 October 2011, 21.00pm.

The Royal Villa, Svolvaer, Grandma arrives.

Sam had played in his workshop all evening. He'd tinkered around and did some more work on his rocket powered chair that he'd flown in the day before in Yorkshire. He'd persuaded Odd and Svend to bring the tatty old chair from Holmford. He'd begged and pleaded and eventually they'd agreed and carried it from the shed and put it in the big boot of the black Mercedes.

Even though he was really tired he was so excited at having lots of good tools, bits of metal, plastic and wood so the time flew by.

At 8 o'clock Jorunn poked her head around the workshop door and called him inside for his dinner, but first she insisted that he have a shower.

"It has been a long day for you Sam," she said, "you've been awake for a lot of hours and you have had lots of shocks and surprises today. And, worst of all, you have been playing in this dirty workshop all evening!"

As he walked into the villa there was only Jorunn about.

"Where is everyone?" asked Sam.

"Hammer has gone to his house in Henningsvaer, he has to go away for a few days. Svend is in his room upstairs, so is Sarah and Odd is in the lounge watching TV. Sam sat down at the table.

"What is this Liten Prinsen?" asked Jorunn, "You need to get washed up! If you hurry up I wont send you to bed without any dinner!"

"You can't do that Jorunn, I'm the new Chieftain!" snapped back Sam quickly, stubbornly not moving from the table.

"Oh Ja! Do you want to try me Sam, maybe you prefer to feel my rolling pin!"

Jorunn looked quite frightening as she opened the drawer that contained a number of heavy looking rolling pins, Sam gulped and decided that it wasn't a good idea to upset her. He got up from the table and rushed upstairs.

"Ja, maybe you are the Liten Prinsen, Sam Marsh," she called as he slumped off to his bedroom, "but you listen to me, in this house, I am the boss!"

Sam had never had a mother or a grandmother before, never had anyone boss him about. He thought about how she'd hugged him earlier, how good it felt being loved, he decided being loved definitely outweighed being told what to do. He'd rather be here, and be wanted, than back in Yorkshire an orphan, all alone in the world.

After Sam had had a shower, he got into a pair of new pyjamas that Jorunn had laid out on his bed for him. He could hear a real commotion coming from downstairs, he could hear a woman shouting in Norwegian and he could hear Jorunn trying to talk to her. Odd was trying to calm the woman down but she sounded upset.

Sam quickly got dressed and crept downstairs try to listen in to the conversation. The problem was they were all talking in Norwegian and he only understood a few words. Sam crept along really stealthily and peeked through a crack in the kitchen door. Inside he could see a woman, she looked old but pretty. Sam thought he knew her from somewhere, thought he recognised her. She didn't look like any of the women in Holmford. She looked like she was a lady or real royalty. She was wearing a long red coat and had white hair. The woman looked really upset. Odd seemed to know her.

Suddenly the women turned around, she spotted Sam peering thought he gap in the door.

"Sam? Sam is that you?" she said, she sounded really posh. She didn't sound Norwegian at all, she sounded English.

The woman rushed out of the kitchen, followed by Odd and Jorunn.

"Hello Sam."

"Er, hello," replied Sam, confused by all the fuss.

"Oh, I've wanted to meet you for so long, I didn't think that this day would come, I really didn't."

"Didn't you?"

"No, no, I thought that I would die without seeing my only great grandson!"

Sam was sat at the kitchen table and Sarah and Svend had joined them. He didn't realise how hungry he was until Jorunn had put a plate of meatballs front of him.

"What're these Jorunn?" asked Sam, "I don't eat meat."

"Ja I know, they're Kjottkaker."

"They're what?"

"Kjottkaker," repeated Jorunn, "Meatballs."

"But I don't eat meat, Jorunn."

"Ja I know they're Vegetarian Kjottkaker!"

"Oh, thanks," Sam thought that he wouldn't be able to eat at all after yet another shock. But he greedily munched on the delicious meal and turned to the visitor. Odd too was munching on some Kjottkaker.

"These are good Sam!" he said, "better than meat Kjottkaker!"

"Yeah, they are," Sam turned to his great grandmother again, he was curious to find out about her, "What is your name again?"

"My name is Freyer Becken, but you can call me Oldemor if you like."

"What does that mean?"

"It means Great Grandma. If you don't want to call me that it's OK."

"I want to. So Oldemor. You are my mum's grandma?"

"Yes Sam. I didn't speak with your mother for a very long time, I wasn't allowed to know her."

"So that means I have another Grandma, your daughter, too?"

"No Sam, I'm sorry she died a long time ago, I'm afraid now you've only got me, my life has been so messy."

"Messy?"

Freyer turned to Odd with a pleading look for him to explain.

"Maybe I can explain what happened Sam." started Odd, wiping his fingers on a tissue, "Do you know that in the war.."

"The second world war?"

"Yeah, in the second world war, Norway was an occupied country? Do you know what that means?"

"Yes, it means that the Germans invaded Norway."

"Yes it does. And anyway those were really difficult times for people in Norway."

"Did the Norwegians not want the Germans to be here?"

"No they did not!" snapped Jorunn, "They did not want to be invaded by the Germans."

"Why?"

"Because," continued Odd, "for invaded, or occupied, countries, life was really hard, terribly hard, people were treated really badly, they couldn't control their own country, they didn't have their own laws. They had to obey German laws."

"Oh. So what happened to you Oldemor?"

Freyer was shocked that Sam had called her Oldemor without even thinking.

"It was a difficult time for my family, I come from an old noble family, we were not used to being told what to do by anybody let alone foreigners. But I was very young, only a teenager, maybe five or six years older than you are now, and when you are young you make the most of life. During the occupation I met a boy."

"A boy? Was this boy your boyfriend?"

"Yes, Sam, he was, he was a kind boy, very clever and very handsome. He was a lot older than me, he was in his twenties but he loved me and I loved him. After the war we were going to get married and have a family."

"Who was this boy?" asked Sam.

Freyer suddenly looked ashamed, she stared down at the floor.

"Oldemor, who was this boy?" Sam was curious.

"He was a German," she whispered.

"A German?"

"Yes, a German, a German officer."

"A captain?" Sam was curious.

"No, he was a high ranking officer, Sam, he was something called a Sturmbannführer..."

Jorunn gasped and sat down, although she wasn't old enough to remember the war her family had told her lots of stories about it.

"What's the matter Jorunn?" asked Sam but Jorunn couldn't speak.

"What's the matter with Jorunn, Odd?" he asked.

"Sturmbannführer was a rank in a special part of the German army, Sam."

"The SS?" Sam knew a lot about the war from Jenny, she was always reading books about it and then telling him all about what went on.

"You know about the SS?" asked Svend.

"Yeah, they were the ones that wore funny black uniforms and were really horrid to everyone. They were bad."

"They were bad, Sam," said Jorunn, "really bad."

Sam casually took another bite of his burger and took a slurp of chocolate soya milk, "So was this boy in the SS Oldemor?"

Freyer gulped and looked straight at Sam.

"You can't help who you fall in love with Sam. Maybe you will realise that one day?"

Freyer explained all about her love affair with the young German officer. How they went on picnics and to dances. She said he was always a gentleman.

"Was he horrible to Norwegian people Oldemor?" asked Sam.

"I never saw him being horrible to people, but I found out a long time later that he wasn't a very nice man."

"What did he do in the army?"

"He was an engineer Sam, a very clever, very special engineer."

"An engineer?" now Sam was very interested, "what sort of engineer?"

"Well I didn't find out too much about what he did, he said it was dangerous for me to know too much."

"But didn't he tell you anything about his work?"

"A little I suppose, his work was something to do with electronics energy and propulsion systems."

"Propulsion?" gasped Sam.

"What's the matter Sam?" asked Freyer a little concerned.

"Freyer," said Svend, "perhaps you'd like to know that Sam is an inventor."

"An inventor?" she said.

"Yes." replied Sam.

"He had us drag one of his inventions all the way from England, he's been working on it in his workshop all evening."

"Sam, I would really like to see your invention, can I come and have a look?" said Freyer.

Sam glanced at Jorunn pleadingly.

"Ja, OK, for five minutes and then you have to go to bed."

"Oh, I'll make sure he's back," said Freyer.

"But what about Oldemor?" asked Sam, "where is she going to stay? She lives a long way away!"

"Don't worry Sam, I'll get a bedroom ready for her, there are plenty of them here, it's a villa after all!"

20) 16 October 2011, 22.30 pm. Deep beneath the North Sea.

X boat 1A was making a steady 35 knots in the cold dark North Sea. It was at a depth of 75 metres and was moving so silently that it was completely undetectable by other submarines and ships. The revolutionary propulsion system of the submarine that had been developed personally by Herr Krater worked supremely silently and, added to this, The Company had developed a special sound insulation skin that meant that even if they held a rock concert on board no sonar commercially available would detect them.

But X boat 1A could hear everything all around it for up to one hundred miles due to its special sonar antenna that spread out all around it like spiders' legs. Conventional submarines rely on a towed array, a large sonar ear that is pulled along on a huge length of wire hundreds of metres long behind the actual submarine. These towed arrays offer excellent listening capabilities. But X boat 1A's spider sonar antennas created an intertwined electronic web that could feel the slightest movement in the ocean for miles and miles, just like a spider feeling a fly land on its web of silk.

On the bridge of the submarine, which was like an underwater space ship, were Commander Herman Bader, Herr Krater and four cyborgs. All was silent as the robots efficiently went about their duties, only needing breaks to interface with their personal hubs every couple of days.

"Disturbance in the web detected, Sir," said a cyborg suddenly in a metallic, inhuman voice.

"Identify," replied Bader.

"British Vanguard class submarine, Sir." replied the cyborg instantly.

"Identify which Vanguard class submarine?" said Bader knowing the information would be instantly available to him, allowing him to make the decisions that other submarine commanders could only dream about.

"HMS Vigilant (S30), Sir."

"Have they detected us?" Bader knew the answer but was showing Herr Krater the excellence of his ship and crew.

"Negative, Sir."

Herr Krater was curious to see just what his fantastic X boat 1A could do, "Why don't you show me what you can do with 1A Commander Bader? Scare HMS Vigilant. Just for fun."

"But sir?" argued Bader feebly.

"Humour me, Commander!" said Krater quietly, "show me what my propulsion system can truly offer the submariner of the twenty first century."

The X boat, as well as moving forward and backward like a traditional sub could move left and right, it could even turn loop the loop and spin underwater. Although it was a vast craft it could turn on the proverbial sixpence if needs be. It also had a weapons system that could destroy the enemy without them even knowing they'd been hit, until it was too late!

"Aye Sir," said Bader, "plot a course to intercept HMS Vigilant," he said to the cyborg at the helm.

"Aye, aye, Sir," answered the robot.

The X boat quickly changed its course and sped through the water at an impressive 60 knots towards the British nuclear boat. Within half an hour X boat 1 A was on a parallel course to HMS Vigilant and had reduced her speed to 20 knots. X boat 1A was only two hundred meters from the starboard side of the Vanguard class submarine and was completely invisible to her, following her every move like a shadow.

"Scare her!" ordered Krater, "Roll her a little."

"Aye Sir," replied Bader.

21) 16 October 2011, 22.57 pm. Bridge of HMS Vigilant.

Commander Duncan Bryce was an experienced submarine commanding officer with four years experience of commanding the magnificent Vanguard class, HMS Vigilant. Built in 1995 she'd just recently been refitted. Her instruments and equipment were all state of the art. At just under 150 metres long, she was a hugely impressive piece of military hardware that represented the front line in Britain's nuclear deterrent. Lurking in the depths of the ocean she thought she was invisible to the world, she was, except to the X boat, which was silently watching her every move.

Executive Officer James Wellborn was five years younger than Bryce, but for the two years that they'd worked together in the cramped confines of this submarine they got along famously. In fact they'd become good friends. Both coming from the north east of England they had developed a good understanding of how the other worked.

Duncan Bryce had just returned to the bridge after a rest break.

"How's everything looking tonight Number One?"

When they were off duty it was always Duncan and James, but on duty they stuck to the strict navy requirements that had served submariners so well since submarines had first come into service in the early years of the twentieth century.

"Everything's calm, Sir," replied Wellborn, "quiet in fact."

HMS Vigilant was headed on a southerly course down through the North Sea, through the straits of Dover and out into the open depths of the Atlantic. She had come the long way round from her home base of Faslaine on the west coast of Scotland.

"Well, that's what we like to hear Number One, calm and quiet!" grinned Bryce.

Suddenly the sixteen thousand tonne boat was rocked fiercely as if there had been a huge underwater earth quake on the sea bed to her starboard side.

"What was that?" shouted Bryce.

"No readings at all on the sonar Sir," replied Sonar man Mike Spears.

The boat was rocked violently again, still from the starboard side.

"What's the reading from the sea bed Sonar?"

"No reading at all."

"No quake?"

"No Sir."

"What on earth was that then?"

"Any damage to any of the systems Number One?"

"No Sir," replied the Executive Officer, "everything completely normal, all systems fully operational."

HMS Vigilant was rocked for a third time this time from the port side.

"Stop all engines!" ordered the Commander.

"All stop!" repeated the Helm.

Another violent blow rocked HMS Vigilant again, this time from the starboard side, ten seconds later a blow to port, ten seconds later, a blow to starboard. The staggering blows went on like this for two minutes, rocking the British boat backwards and forward. Suddenly they were knocked from the front, then the back, then the front again.

"Action stations!" called Bryce.

"Action stations, Sir!" repeated XO.

Suddenly all the external forces stopped and HMS Vigilant was sat still in the water, 75 metres below the surface of the North Sea. All was quiet and calm once again. It was as if nothing had happened.

"Blow all tanks and surface! Take her up!" called Bryce as the submarine remained on red alert, "Periscope depth!"

"Aye, aye Sir!" replied the helm, "taking her up. Periscope depth."

As HMS Vigilant rose quickly to just below the surface she didn't detect her silent assailant moving away quickly through the water and diving deep.

"Periscope depth Sir," called the Helm.

"Periscope up!" ordered Commander Bryce.

"Periscope up sir."

Commander Bryce slowly and carefully turned 360 degrees but could see nothing through the night vision binoculars of the periscope. There were no other vessels on the horizon.

"No sight of anything. Must have been some kind of systems malfunction," concluded Bryce, scratching his head, as he peered through the periscope, "Put a full report into HQ Number One, tell them everything, and make a course change, we're returning to base! Straight away! We need to get this checked out!"

22) 17 October 2011, 1.00 am. X boat 1A

X boat 1A had followed HMS Vigilant for a couple of hours following the incident and Herr Krater had just returned to the bridge after resting in his spacious cabin.

"What's the update on our British friends Commander?"

"They are returning to base Sir, they put in a report to their headquarters reporting the entire incident, they think that they have had a major technological problem Sir."

"Incompetent idiots, sailing around the oceans in their pieces of outdated junk. They have closed minds Bader, relying merely on *tried and tested* technology instead of looking to the future."

"Yes Sir," agreed Bader, "this boat and the others in the fleet are truly the masters of the ocean."

"Yes Bader, they are, and when we get to the Helmsfjord and get those plans back then The Company will be the masters of the air too, we will make the jet engine look like an elastic band. When we develop that engine then space travel will be revolutionised!"

"Aye Sir."

"The human race visited the moon forty years ago and since then, what?"

Bader shrugged.

"Then nothing Commander Bader, nothing! Twenty five years of the shuttle, men and women sat on top of millions of litres of rocket fuel. Riding into space on the front of a gigantic firework when they could have been colonising the moons of Jupiter or Saturn! Do you know Bader, that when we develop our new propulsion system an intergalactic ship will be able to travel to Mars in just a couple of hours. How long do you think it would take using conventional rockets Bader?"

"I..I don't know sir," replied Commander Bader.

"Well, using the Hohman Transfer Orbit, which is the traditional mainstay of interplanetary space travel, when Mars and the Earth are at their closest points, which happens every 1.6 years, it will take 260 days, give or take!" Krater laughed, "We, Commander Bader, have just started with this toy we're aboard, your fantastically amazing X boat is just a toy, and we've only just started!"

23) 17 October 2011, 9.00 am. The Royal Villa, breakfast.

Sam was so excited about waking up in a new place that he didn't sleep in late and by 9 o'clock he was washed, dressed, in the kitchen and ready to have some breakfast and then to do some exploring around his new home. Freyer, Odd and Svend were already sat around the large kitchen table eating breakfast and drinking strong black coffee. He hated the taste of coffee but he loved the smell and he could smell it even before he got downstairs.

"Morning!" said Sam breezily as he danced into the kitchen.

"Good morning," they all replied.

"Morning Oldemor," he said kissing his Great Grandma on the cheek.

"Hello Sam," she replied a little surprised, "did you sleep well?"

"Yeah, great," replied Sam inspecting what was on offer, "Where's Sarah?"

"Oh, she's still asleep, I think she must be really tired." replied Svend, "yesterday must have taken its toll on her!"

"But I'm OK!" exclaimed Sam.

"You're just a boy Sam," explained Freyer, "you've got bundles of energy!"

"What's for breakfast Jorunn?" asked Sam.

"Oh, there's all sorts Sam, in Norway people like a lot of choice at breakfast time."

"Pancakes and waffles?" he asked hopefully.

"We don't normally eat pancakes and waffles for breakfast Sam, that's for coffee time in the afternoon," said Svend, "In the morning we have lots of bits and pieces. Why don't you go and help yourself, there's lot of tasty things to choose from."

On a large breakfast bar to the side of the table were all kinds of foods, boiled eggs, sliced cucumber, sliced tomatoes, lots of different kinds of bread and big funny blocks of funny looking butter. Sam loaded his plate up with some cucumber, tomato and eggs, some pieces of bread and some blobs of jam. But he looked suspiciously at the strange coloured butter stuff.

"What's that funny looking butter stuff?" he asked cautiously.

"It's cheese Sam," explained Freyer.

"Ja," said Jorunn, "that brown cheese is called Gjetost. Use that peeler over there and peel off some slices Sam, then you can put it on your bread."

"It doesn't taste at all like English cheese Sam," said Odd, "it's sweeter."

"Sweeter? Sweet cheese?" Sam pulled a face.

"Well you do have sweet cheesy things in England too, Sam, what about cheesecakes?" explained Odd.

"Cheescakes? I never thought that they were made of cheese."

"Well they are," added Freyer, "and they're sweet. Try some of that Gjetost Sam, you might like it."

Sam sliced off some of the brown cheese smelled it suspiciously and placed it on a slice of bread.

"Mmm, it's quite nice, very, very.."

"Caramelly!" said Odd.

"Yeah, it tastes like Caramac chocolate bars," said Sam.

"Yeah it does!" agreed Odd, "I like them too."

"Vil du ha en kaffe tår?" asked Jorunn forgetting Sam couldn't speak much Norwegian.

"What?" said Sam his mouth full.

"Jorunn, remember, Sam doesn't speak Norwegian," said Freyer.

"Oh, sorry Sam, would you like a drop of coffee?"

"Coffee? No thanks," said Sam, "can I have some chocolate soya milk?"

"Ja, for sure."

As Sam finished his breakfast he politely looked at Jorunn.

"Jorunn, can I go and play in my workshop?"

"Well I think Svend and Odd wanted to show you around the island, but the weather is very bad. So.." she looked at Svend.

"Yeah, you can go to the workshop, the weather is too bad at the moment, but we have to go into town before lunch, we are meeting some very special people."

"OK," said Sam as he left the table.

Sam had made some big adjustments to his rocket chair the previous evening. He'd increased the size of the fuel tanks, built bigger thrusters and had wired up a rudder that allowed him to steer the chair.

As well as the big chair he'd also brought his model chair and his Action Man from England. All through the design process Sam had made sure that for every adjustment he made to the big chair he made exactly the same one for the small model. He was very careful. He read a book once by an inventor that said how important it was to test your design properly before you tried it on people. That way nobody got hurt if something went wrong. So Sam had made all the adjustments to the model as he had to the arm chair.

"What are you doing Sam?" said a woman's voice from the door.

"Oh, Oldemor!" said Sam a little startled, "I didn't see you there, you shocked me!"

"Sorry. But I've been watching you for quite a while Sam, you're very clever you know."

"Thanks."

"What is it you're building now?"

"The rocket chair."

"The rocket chair?"

"Yeah, and it flies too!" said Sam.

"How do you know that?"

"Because I've flown in it."

"Have you? Actually flown in it?"

"Well it didn't fly exactly, but it did lift off the ground, two metres off the ground!"

"Two metres? That's high! You know you should be very careful Sam."

"Yeah, I always am, I've got safety gear and everything."

"That's very sensible. Why didn't it fly higher than two metres?"

"Oh I don't think that I got the fuel mix right."

"What fuel are you using?" Freyer was really interested in everything he did.

"It's a mix of sugar and potassium nitrate," explained Sam.

"Is it?"

"Yeah, some people call it rocket candy."

"Really? Rocket candy?"

"Yeah. It's true, here have a look at this website," Sam took his computer over to Freyer and she had a good look at the website, "But since I flew in it last I've developed bigger fuel storage tanks, more powerful rockets and a way of controlling where you're going."

"Well, controlling where you're going is a very good idea!"

"Do you want to see me test my model out, Oldemor?"

"Oh, yes please."

Sam carefully took the model chair and strapped his action man gently into it. He even placed a small helmet over his head and secured it! Sam took the chair and placed it at the far end of the workshop. Picking up a remote control he went to stand with Freyer.

"Do you want to do the countdown in Norwegian for me Oldemor?"

"Yes OK, are you ready?"

"Ready!"

"OK, fem, fire, tre, to, en, null!"

Sam pressed the big red button on the remote control and the small rocket chair started hissing and puffing, the noise got louder and louder and suddenly flames erupted from the rockets and the rocket chair shot up off the ground. Sam was a bit startled because it took off so fast but he quickly regained control. Expertly he steered the little chair with the action man in round and round the room. This way and that it flew.

"It's so manoeuvrable!" shouted Freyer over the noise of the rocket engines, which were loud.

"Yeah! I know!"

"How long can it stay in the air?"

"This model can't stay up long, a few minutes, but the big chair can fly for about one hour, I think."

"One hour? That's a long time."

"Yeah, I know. Maybe it can fly for longer when I get better fuel?"

Expertly Sam steered the small model back towards the landing pad and gradually reduced the speed.

"Coming in to land Oldemor!" he shouted, a big grin all over his face.

Sam landed the model on the landing pad and rushed over to the model to switch off the engines. It was so quiet after the engines had been turned off.

"Oh, I think I have gone deaf!" laughed Freyer.

"Sorry!"

"No, no don't be sorry Sam, it's brilliant, and you have done all this by yourself?"

"Well Jenny and Spike helped me build the chairs, but I designed them."

Freyer reached over and hugged Sam tightly, "You are a very, very clever young man Sam, and I am very proud of you."

24) 17 October 2011, 13.00. The Royal villa surprise visitors, Jenny and Spike arrive!

After grabbing a veggie ham sandwich, Sam, along with Svend, Odd and Sarah got into the Range Rover and headed out of the guarded house.

"Bye Sam!" called the guards.

"Bye!" waved Sam as he passed.

"That veggie ham tastes just like real ham, Sam," said Odd licking his lips.

"Odd, do you ever think about anything else but food?" asked Sarah.

"Not too often," he replied then got back to the subject in hand, "but *that* veggie ham!"

"Yeah it does, so there's no need for you to eat meat from animals now Odd," replied Sam firmly. Sam was a committed vegetarian, he couldn't bear the thought that people killed animals for food.

"No there isn't, is there," agreed Odd.

"Can we get this ham in Norway, Svend?" asked Odd.

"Yeah I think so, definitely in Oslo, we'll have to go down to the Coop or Rimi here in Svolaer to make sure they have a good selection."

"I could order them to stock it!" said Sam

"Yeah, you could!" agreed Svend.

The Range Rover drove across the stunning island and Sam thought he recognised where he was going.

"Where are we going Svend?"

"It's a surprise," said Svend.

"Oh."

The scenery was so dramatic, there were huge mountains rising thousands of feet into the air and rugged cliffs. Sam peered up but because of the bad weather, it was still raining and the sea was still very stormy, he couldn't see the tops of the peaks. They were covered in thick cloud.

"Does it always ran like this in Svolvaer?" asked Sam.

"Not always," said Svend, "but October is the rainiest month, and as you can see, we do get a lot of rain in October!"

Following the E10 road out of Svolvaer, the Range Rover meandered its way around the pretty coastal road, passing groups of red coloured houses dotted her and there. Almost every house on the coast had its own small jetty with a boat moored to it.

"There are a lot of boats!" said Sam.

"Nearly everyone in Lofoten has a boat Sam," explained Svend, "the sea is really important for a small group of islands like ours. All through history the sea has been important to us. Hammer told me that there was a man who lives in the house next to the villa, an old artist, he knows everything about the history of Lofoten, Hammer said you should pop in and see him sometime, he said you'd love the stories he can tell!"

"Does he speak English, Svend?"

"Yeah, he speaks lots of languages."

As they drove along the coast road suddenly the airport came into view.

"The airport!" said Sam, "Are we going flying again today."

"No, Sam, not today," said Odd.

"Then why are we here?"

"It's a surprise."

"Are we going to see another interesting plane Odd? Is that why we're here?"

"Wait and see!"

The Range Rover was waved straight through security and made its way to the private area of the airport where it sat waiting. The rain was still beating down.

"What are we waiting for?" asked Sam.

"For that!" said Odd peering through the windscreen.

Far into the distance Sam could see a tiny light. As he stared he could see that it was getting brighter and brighter. Gradually out of the thick rain clouds appeared a distant plane. It gradually got closer and closer and banked steeply to get into the right position to land.

"It's the Aerion SBJ!" cheered Sam.

"Yeah!" agreed Odd.

"Wow it's so fantastic!"

"Yep!" agreed Odd.

The sleek Aerion SBJ came in towards the runway and landed smoothly. It slowed down and started coming towards them. Sam gawped at the small supersonic jet. The plane came to a halt close to their car and the engines were switched off.

"Sam! Sam!"

Sam could hear someone calling his name. When he looked he saw Captain Harket hanging out of the cockpit window waving at him.

"No problems today Sam!" he shouted

Sam wound down his window and called back.

"No Genies?"

"No, no Genies today," laughed the captain.

The airport staff pushed some stairs upto the jet and Anita and Hilde opened the cabin door.

"Hi Sam!" they waved.

"Hi Anita, Hi Hilde!" called Sam back.

Suddenly two familiar figures, huddled up in thick coats appeared next to the two stewardesses.

"Jenny! Spike!" called Sam, "It's Jenny and Spike," he said to the others in the car.

"Yes, we know," said Sarah.

"Sam!" called Jenny excitedly, "Sam!"

"Alright, Sam!" called Spike not wanting to look too uncool, his mop of hair becoming plastered to his head because he

137

didn't want to put his hood up, especially not in the presence of the glamorous Anita and Hilde!

Jenny pulled her hood tightly around her tied back red hair and started skipping down the stairs. Sam got out of the car and ran towards her.

"Sam, it's great to see you!" she sobbed, Sam had never seen Jenny cry, ever, she was far too tough!

"It's great to see you to!" said Sam, "But I've only been gone for one day you know!"

"Yeah I know, but the place just wasn't the same without you."

"Has Jessie not come?" said Sam looking around Jenny.

"No, she hates flying, remember."

"That and the fact that they wouldn't fit her on a plane, well not that plane, it's too small!" laughed Sam.

"Yeah, they'd need a jumbo jet for Jessie Brooks!" agreed Jenny.

"Alright Sam," said Spike reaching out to shake his friend's hand, "nice to see you mate. Neat plane that!"

"Yeah, it's fantastic, do you know what it is?"

"An Aerion I think but I don't know which, it looks pretty new though."

"Yeah it's brand new, and it's actually an Aerion SBJ!"

"An SBJ? I didn't know they were on the market yet," said Spike.

"They're not, not properly, this is the first."

"The first?"

"Yeah."

"Wicked! Must have a cost a lot of dough?"

"Yeah, 80 million dollars!"

"80 million dollars!" Spike nearly fell over, "flippin' 'eck that must be a lot of knocks!"

"Knocks?" asked Sam a little confused, "what's a knock?"

"You know, the knock," continued Spike.

"No Spike we don't know, what on earth is a knock?" asked Jenny.

"You know the *knock*!"

"No we don't!" said Sam and Jenny together, "tell us what you're talking about!"

"The Knock!" repeated Spike as if Jenny and Sam were mad.

"Spike," Jenny was losing her temper, and Spike was in physical danger.

"Spike you'd better explain," said Sam stepping in, "the only knock's I know about are the ones in front of those knock, knock jokes!"

But Spike couldn't understand why his friends couldn't understand what he was talking about. Instead he got out an envelope that he'd got before he took off from Leeds Airport.

"There! Look!" he pointed to some words on the envelope. "*Noks!*"

Sam and Jenny looked at the envelope with had the words "Bureau de change" in big letters on the top, underneath were numbers. Suddenly it dawned on them what he was talking about.

"You are a twonk, Spike!" laughed Jenny pushing Spike.

"Why? What have I done now?" Spike didn't know what they were talking about.

"It's not *knock* Spike," explained Sam, "it's *Nok*!"

"*Knock*, that's what I said."

"Spike, knock is something you do on a door before someone answers it," explained Jenny laughing, "NOK is N. O. K. it means Norwegian Krona, that's the money here."

"Yeah, Spike," continued Sam trying to explain, "when people buy American money they call it dollars but it's written down on the bureau de change papers as USD. But people don't say UZZD," Sam enjoyed making the sound, "they say US dollars! Jenny's right Spike you are a twonk!"

"Mop twonk!" added Jenny.

"Yeah," chuckled Spike "I suppose I am, UZZD, I like that one! I think I'm going to be a Wall Street trader when I grow up," he joked, " except I'm gonna trade in UZZD's!"

25) 17 October 2011, 14.00 Unterwasserwelt moves slowly down the Norwegian coast.

The world had not seen anything on the scale of Unterwasserwelt, which was German for underwater world. And as it spent all its time on the floor of the world's oceans nobody would ever see it unless something catastrophic occurred and everyone involved in the project said that was impossible.

The undersea base was a giant five pronged starfish shape which from the tip of each leg to the centre measured just over 500 metres. This made Unterwasserwelt a vast moving military machine, the second biggest machine ever built by man, the space station being currently constructed by The Company on the dark side of the moon being the biggest.

Specifically built to allow the X boats to dock with her and use her as a base, Underwasserwelt was designed so that one huge X boat could dock on either side of her legs when she was stationary, meaning that a maximum of ten X boats could dock with the base at any one time.

Being so large it was a miracle that the Unterwasserwelt moved at all, but move she did albeit very slowly. She was currently just crawling past the Norwegian Northern Cape, the most northerly part of mainland Europe. It would take her two more days of crawling 24/7 to reach her destination of the Lofoten Islands.

Commander Dirk Reich was in charge of this naval miracle. A dashing young former German sailor, top in all his classes, he was the best of the best, the creme de la creme. Sailors did not get any better than Reich. So when The Company had approached him secretly two years ago with an exciting new commercial venture he'd been more than interested and happy to meet with Herr Krater personally in Berlin.

Reich was married to his job and he loved everything about being a submariner, in fact in his spare time he took vacations where he knew the diving was first class. Dirk Reich just loved being underwater.

But everything about the job application had been shrouded in secrecy. It was a very strange experience that Reich could tell no-one about. It had all started when he got a vague text on his mobile phone whilst he was on shore leave a couple of years ago.

"R U interested in a new job?" had been the first text.

"No, not really!" replied Reich thinking that that would be the end of the matter, but he was wrong.

A few minutes later another text arrived, Reich was curious and he was hooked.

"Wait for the next text and look at the web page you are given," was all it had said.

When the next text came Dirk was so curious he couldn't wait to fire up his dusty old laptop and take a look. And what he saw on that web page changed his life forever. It showed plans, plans for something so mind boggling he couldn't stop thinking about it. Shortly after logging on a man called him on his mobile.

"Do you like what you see Herr Reich?" asked the man's voice vaguely.

"Er, yeah, yeah I do, but I don't understand, who are you? What do you want from me?"

"Achtung! Listen carefully! You will receive a text message shortly, note the address and be there tomorrow morning at nine sharp. Bring an overnight bag."

"But.." said Reich trying to glean more information but the phone had already gone dead. He looked down at his phone and tried to bring up the details of the call, but all the phone said was "No number listed."

Dirk Reich looked up the address when it arrived in the next text and carefully worked out how he would get there the next morning. He decided to take a cab and when he arrived at the address he was shocked to discover it was a fast food restaurant. He wandered in not knowing if the whole thing had been a bizarre joke or not.

"Can I help you sir?" asked the girl behind the counter.

"Er, I don't know," stuttered Reich.

"Are you Herr Reich? Herr Dirk Reich?" asked the young woman.

"Er, yeah, yes I am."

"Well Sir, you are expected, if you would just go through to the back, go straight passed the toilets, someone is down there waiting for you."

"What, just down there?" pointed Reich.

"Yes, that's right Sir," smiled the girl.

Reich was deeply suspicious but once again his curiosity got the better of him and he followed the instructions the girl had given him. As he walked through to the back of the restaurant suddenly he felt a dull thud on the back of his head and he was out cold, knocked out.

When Dirk Reich awoke he was laid on a bed in a small hospital room, completely unsure of where he was. His head throbbed terribly and when he looked down he discovered that he was wearing pyjamas. He was connected up to machines that were monitoring his vital signs. There were no windows in the room and for some reason Reich got the feeling he was on a ship. There was no feeling of movement, no drone of any engines, but somehow it just felt like a room on a ship, small and cramped.

Reich reached out and pressed what he thought was an intercom button, "Hello!" he called and an electronic voice spoke to him.

"Please stay where you are Herr Reich and someone will be with you momentarily."

Reich waited for a couple of minutes and then the door slid open to reveal an elderly doctor and a young blond female nurse.

"Welcome back Herr Reich," said the doctor, "We were quite concerned when you just collapsed on us!"

"Collapsed? I don't remember collapsing."

"What actually is the last thing you do recall?" asked the doctor as he checked all the instruments that Reich was attached to.

"Er, I don't know exactly," things were a blur for Reich as he struggled to remember, "er, I remember going into a restaurant and then nothing, darkness, and then I just woke up here."

"Ah?" said the Doctor disconnecting him.

"Well?" said Reich, "Am I OK?"

"Yes, yes, you are perfectly well Herr Reich."

"Where exactly am I, doctor?"

"Herr Krater will explain everything to you."

"But where am I?"

"I'm afraid I cannot answer your questions, I am not authorised to do so, now if you will forgive me I have other patients to attend to."

And with that the doctor left the room and left Dirk Reich alone with the young nurse.

"Can you tell me anything?" he asked her, but she didn't respond.

"Excuse me?" said Reich trying to get the woman's attention, "Excuse me?" he nudged her arm to try and get her attention. She felt cold, ice cold, like a piece of metal. She looked up at him and her eyes, they were like miniature computer screens, tiny scrolls of writing were whizzing across her lenses like a computer monitor.

"What?" stuttered Reich, "What are you?"

"She is a robot Herr Reich," said a man's voice from the door way.

When Reich looked up there was an old man stood in the doorway, he hadn't noticed him before so he must have just come in.

"Who are you?" asked Reich.

"My name is Herr Krater, I am the president of The Company."

"What company?"

"Just *The* Company, you could say we are quite a low profile organisation, but please do not let that fool you, we are far reaching in our scope, vision and impact."

"But I've never heard of them."

"I'm glad to hear you haven't Herr Reich, that would be a disastrous situation for us and you!

"What do you mean by that?" Reich was starting to feel very uncomfortable.

"Nothing, nothing at all."

"Where I am Herr?"

"Krater."

"Herr Krater, it feels like I'm on board a ship."

"Well, Herr Reich in a way you are. Herr Reich, would you forgive me if we got straight down to business, I am rather a busy man."

"Fine," replied Reich hoping that he might get some answers, shed some light on the most bizarre situation of his entire life.

"Herr Reich, I understand you were intrigued by one particular website you visited recently?"

"The underwater world?"

Herr Krater nodded.

"Yeah, definitely, the possibility of developing an underwater military base in the future is something that definitely interests me. But what has that got to do with me being here?"

"Well Herr Reich you are a very highly regarded submariner."

"Yes, I know," replied Reich modestly.

"Maybe the best of the very best some would say."

"Would they?"

"They would."

"So?" Reich wanted to stop the cat and mouse games, "Herr Krater, would you just mind coming straight to the point, I'm not a big fan of silly mind games."

"Very well," Herr Krater walked across the room and sat down in a chair beside the bed, "Leave us!" he ordered the nurse who immediately left the room without answering, "Herr Reich, the plans for the underwater base are not merely plans, they are reality."

"Reality?" Reich was stunned.

"What would you say if I told you that you were on board Unterwasserwelt this very moment Herr Reich?"

"I would say that you were having me on!" he laughed.

Krater leaned from his chair and pressed a few buttons on a key pad on the wall, suddenly the wall slid down revealing a huge floor to ceiling window looking out onto an underwater kingdom. Through the murky water Reich could see giant submarines drifting slowly past and divers working on a huge underwater construction site.

"Granted, it is not yet operational," said Krater as Reich stared open mouthed, "but it is the world's first Unterwasserwelt!"

The chance of not only working on the fantastic Unterwasserwelt but commanding it was just too great a lure for Dirk Reich. Within the hour he'd signed a one million dollars a year employment deal and half a million dollars had been deposited in his bank account as a golden 'hello'. He resigned his post with the navy that very day and within two months he was back on board the undersea base and helping finalise its completion. Now he was commanding it on its first mission. Proceed to the Norwegian Lofoten Islands and wait for the arrival of Herr Krater, those had been his vague instructions and that was what he was doing.

26) 17 October 2011, 14.30. Exploring the Royal Villa with friends.

"Wow, neat car!" exclaimed Spike as they got into the black Range Rover.

"Thanks!" replied Sam a little smugly.

"Does it always rain in the Lofoten Islands?" asked Jenny as the rain started to beat down once more.

"Not all the time," replied Svend as he drove out of the airport and back towards Svolvaer, the airport was a short drive out of the town, "but we do tend to get rather a lot in the autumn time and as I was telling Sam earlier, October is the wettest month."

"Actually," joined in Odd, "Svolvaer being on the eastern side of the islands tends to get quite a bit less rain than some of the more exposed western parts."

"Wicked!" said Spike, "they must be like Mer-people or something then?"

"Maybe!" laughed Odd.

"But it is a very beautiful place, Lofoten," added Jenny as the late afternoon dusk began to slowly fall over the islands.

"Hey Sam, you must be really important!" gasped Spike as they drove through the gates with the armed guards.

"I suppose," mused Sam, getting used to the security.

They drove along the long road upto the villa and as they rounded a bend even Sam got his first proper look at the villa in the daylight. The day before it had been dark when they'd arrived and he hadn't been able to get a good look at it this morning either.

The villa was a huge wooden building. Three floors and spread out over a large surface area, it was painted rust red and looked like a much glorified holiday cabin or old fashioned hotel. Apparently, he was told, this was the height of luxury and he wasn't complaining!

But the setting of the house was more impressive than the house itself. The villa overlooked dramatic sea cliffs and there were long green fields that ran all the way to its own private cliff top.

"Wow Sam, is this your new home?" asked Jenny.

"Yeah."

"Neat place!" added Spike.

"Yeah, thanks."

"Is that a private beach over there?" pointed Jenny.

"I don't know, is it Svend?" asked Sam.

"Yes it is Sam, and there is a private jetty too and.."

"And," butted in Odd, "there's a private speed boat moored to it!"

"A speed boat?"

"Yeah, a neat one too, wait til you get to see it, it's awesome, it's got sailors and everything!"

As the car pulled up to the house Jorunn and Freyer came out to meet them. Sam got out of the car and to the astonishment of Jenny and Spike, and even Freyer, ran over to his Great Grandma and flung his arms around her.

"Spike, Jenny, come here will you, I want you to meet Oldemor!"

"Oldemor?" asked Jenny.

"Yeah, that means Great Grandma in Norwegian!" explained Sam.

"Great Grandma? This is your Great Grandma?" asked Jenny.

"When did you find out you had a Great Grandma?" asked Spike.

"Yesterday," replied Sam.

"Oldemor, these are my friends Spike Williams and Jenny James, Spike, Jenny this is my Great Grandma, Freyer Becken."

"Hello Spike, hello Jenny," said Freyer shaking the hands of Sam's surprised friends, "nice to meet you."

"Yeah, er hi," said Spike.

"Hello," said Jenny a little suspiciously.

"Spike is a computer whizz, sometimes we call him Mop, because of his hair. Jenny is the cleverest person I know, she's into history, she knows the history of almost anything."

"Lovely," said Freyer.

"And everyone," continued Sam, "this is Jorunn, she takes care of everything, she's the boss of the house."

"Hello you two! Come on in, you must be hungry!" said Jorunn.

"Well, I am come to think of it!" said Spike who loved his food almost as much as Odd!

Sam showed Jenny and Spike to their separate bedrooms, which had their own bathrooms attached, televisions, computers and a telephone. He told them to come downstairs as soon as they were ready because Jorunn was making some afternoon tea.

Spike was the first to bound downstairs, the lure of the smell of cooking pancakes making him move remarkably quickly.

"Great stuff!" he said as he walked into the kitchen," afternoon tea!"

"We don't really have afternoon tea in Norway, Spike," said Jorunn dishing out a fresh pancake for him "in Norway we have afternoon coffee."

"Coffee in the afternoon?" asked Spike.

"Ja, we drink coffee all day in Norway," added Jorunn, "would you like some, or maybe you would prefer some homemade lemonade instead?"

"Homemade lemonade please," mumbled Spike as he started eating the pancake without anything on it.

"You can put something on your pancake if you like Spike," said Odd, "some maple syrup maybe, or some sour cream, maybe some jam or honey, that's my favourite, honey, I love it!"

"Er, is there any chocolate sauce?" asked Spike.

"Sure," said Odd passing him some, "we have everything here in Norway."

Sam was also munching on a pancake, his with maple syrup on top, when Jenny came walking into the room, Sam could see that she wasn't as happy as Spike. Something was upsetting her.

"Would you like something to eat Jenny?" asked Jorunn.

"No thank you."

"Maybe a drink then?"

"Just some orange juice please."

"What's the matter Jenny?" asked Sarah, who was sipping a cup of tea.

"Nothing," said Jenny as she sipped her orange.

"There is, tell me, what is it?"

"I don't want to talk about it," she mumbled, suddenly she got up from the table and shot out of the room.

Sam ran after her and Sarah got up to follow but Freyer grabbed her arm and stopped her.

"Leave them Sarah, it's me, Jenny's not happy about me being here. It's a big shock to her."

Jenny had gone outside and had walked around to the back of the house where there was large covered veranda with seats and tables. Although it was still raining it was dry on the veranda.

"Here you are," said Sam as he found her.

"Yeah, here I am," mumbled Jenny, she was upset.

"What's the matter Jen?"

"Nothing."

"Tell me! It's something? What is it?"

"I said it's nothing!" snapped Jenny.

Sam sat quietly for a few moments.

"It Freyer isn't it?" he said quietly.

"No!"

"It is Jenny! I know you too well, I know when you're upset about something and I know that it's Freyer you're upset about."

Sam was right, Jenny was not only upset about Freyer being back in Sam's life she was a little jealous too.

"Oh, alright!" she snapped again, "It is Freyer, walking back into your life after all these years!"

"She didn't walk back," said Sam, "I didn't even know she existed before yesterday, and she didn't know about me either."

"And you just let her back in, Great Grandma this, Great Grandma that!"

"Oldemor!" corrected Sam.

"OK! Oldemor this and Oldemor that!"

"Jenny!"

"Don't Jenny me! For years we've all three stuck together when there's been no one else and now she's here when you're made the new king or whatever it is that you are!"

"It's not like that, Jenny!"

"What is it like then?"

"Well it's like this, Jenny," Freyer had walked around the back of the house to join them.

Freyer started explaining her entire history. About meeting and falling in love with a German SS officer and then being betrayed by him. Lots of things she spoke about she hadn't told Sam yet so he was listening quietly too.

"But when the war was finished and he disappeared I discovered that I was pregnant," said Freyer honestly.

"With Sam's grandmother?" asked Jenny.

"Yes, with my daughter, Agnes, and can you imagine what sort of situation that was for a young woman at the time in Norway, a country that did not want to be occupied, that did not like the Germans, that hated the SS in particular.

Jenny was thoughtful for a while then spoke quietly, "Not very good?"

"Worse than not very good Jenny, it was bad, dangerous in fact. Lots of Norwegians naturally wanted revenge and they were determined to get it from girls like me, and believe me I wasn't the only one."

"No?" asked Jenny.

"No, there were thousands of girls in the same situation as me, but maybe it was even worse for them because my family had plenty of money."

"So what did you do, Oldemor?"

"I did the only thing I could, I ran!" Freyer paused for a minute, "awful things were happening to girls like me, and I just couldn't face up to it," she started crying gently, "maybe I was a coward, I don't know, but I couldn't face what they would do to me. And I really wanted my baby to be safe."

"So where did you run to, Freyer?" asked Jenny.

"I went with my mother to distant relatives in southern Sweden, there was not a problem there and we were able to make a new life for us with our cousins near Malmo."

"And the father, Sam's Great Grandfather did you ever see him again?" asked Jenny.

"No, I've haven't seen him since the war."

"Is he dead?" asked Sam curiously.

Freyer paused, "No Sam, he's not dead, after the war he became a very eminent scientist, he had a very successful career, even won the Nobel prize for his work on engines or something..."

At this last bit Sam's ears pricked up.

"..and then he formed one of the biggest companies in the world, some people think he's dead but he's still well and truly alive. But he is a very secretive man. But I hope I will never meet him ever again."

"What's his name?" asked Sam.

"Sam, you don't want to have anything to do with your Great Grandfather," pleaded Freyer, "please trust me, keep well away from him."

"Why?"

"Believe me, I know all about him, about what he does Sam, I've had investigators spy on him, he is a very, very nasty man."

"Please Oldemor, tell me his name?"

"Freyer, he has a right to know, he's not a child you know," said Jenny seriously.

Freyer thought long and hard and then spoke again.

"Eric Krater," she said quietly, "his name is Eric Krater, and he's the president of an organisation called The Company."

"Eric Krater," repeated Sam quietly to himself.

"Yes. But remember, I've warned you about him Sam!" said Freyer quietly, "stay away from him, I beg you! Please!"

27) 17 October 2011, 18.00. The bridge of Unterwasserwelt.

"What is your position Commander Reich?" asked Herr Krater speaking to him on the video link.

"We are well passed the North Cape Sir, we are on schedule, our estimated time of arrival at the rendezvous point is 1600 hours 18 October, 46 hours from now."

"Excellent. Has there been any naval activity to report?"

"Nothing out of the ordinary Sir, just one Borei class Russian submarine returning to base."

"Which one was it Reich?"

"The Alexander Nevsky Sir."

"The new boat?"

"Yes Sir, it has just completed its sea trials, I understand."

"You're correct Reich, how far is she from Unterwasserwelt at the moment?"

"Twenty miles Sir."

"Is she within reach of the ESD?"

"The electronic scrambling device?"

"Yes, Reich.

"She is, sir."

"Then scramble her systems Reich, send her back into dry dock for another month or two just for good luck!"

"But, Sir, she is in international waters and she has made no attempt to engage us at all."

"She can't even see you, Reich," laughed Krater, "just scramble the Alexander Nevsky, Reich, use it as a test run of our scrambling device."

"Aye sir."

Commander Reich checked on the exact position of the Alexander Nevsky, fortunately she was on the surface so there would be no casualties from his actions. But he wasn't happy about what he was about to do.

"Plot the exact position of the Alexander Nevsky!" he called to his weapons android.

"Aye sir. Course plotted!" replied the robot.

"Feed her co-ordinates into the ESD."

"Co-ordinates fed into ESD, Sir."

"Activate scrambler!"

"Scrambler activated, Sir."

28) 17 October 2011, 18.10. The bridge of the RFS Alexander Nevsky.

The immense Borei class nuclear powered submarine, the RFS Alexander Nevsky, had just completed its rigorous months of sea trials. All the systems had been checked, double checked and triple checked. Nothing had been left to chance, it couldn't be when they spent most of their time underwater where the smallest of mistake could cost lives. There had been a small amount of fine tuning to do but now the boat was working magnificently.

RFS Alexander Nevsky was the third of twelve boats to be completed in this Borei class and they were lethal war machines. Lurking in the depths of the ocean, unbeknown to the world, they could go where they wanted, they stayed underwater for months at a time, they could use their 16 new, lethal Bulava SBLM (Submarine Launched Ballistic Missiles) to carry nuclear warheads to attack any city in the world, causing complete destruction at the merest press of a button.

A huge boat, one of the biggest ever built, she was 170 metres long and weighed over fourteen thousand tonnes. With a crew of 130, Captain Second Rank Dimitri Antipova was just the man to be granted the great honour of the top job of commanding this state of the art weapon.

"Nearly home, Sir!" laughed First Officer Yuri Bartnev as they enjoyed a couple of minutes alone after a busy few months conducting the rigorous sea trials.

"It's been a long one for sure, Yuri," replied Antipova. It was like the last day at school on board the Alexander Nevsky and now the crew had the prospect of three weeks shore leave ahead of them.

Antipova and Bartnev were stood outside on the top of the huge tower enjoying some fresh air.

"What do you think, Sir?" asked Bartnev.

"Mm? About what Yuri?"

"About how she's performed in the sea trials Sir?"

"I think that we are very lucky sailors, I think we've got ourselves one fantastic piece of Russian engineering, we'll be the envy of the Russian navy in this boat and, once again, the world will respect the military might of Mother Russia."

"She's fantastic, isn't she?"

"She is Yuri, she's one fantastic boat."

Suddenly everything stopped. The boats turbines stopped turning, all the electronics went off line, the computers went down, there was nothing, the Alexander Nevsky was dead in the water. She had no propulsion, no controls, nothing. It was just a matter of time until the life support systems went off line too. She was dead.

"What the....." shouted Antipova, "What's happened?"

"There's no intercom, Sir," said Bartnev, "no electronics at all, everything's dead." he bent down and shouted through the hatch, "what's going on down there, Helm?"

"Don't know sir, we have no power, we've gone on to auxiliary batteries, but we're operating on a very skeletal system."

"What's the situation with the reactor?" shouted a worried Bartnev. The Alexander Nevsky was powered by the limitless power of a OK-650 pressurized water nuclear reactor. If anything happened to that then they were all dead, either very quickly if she went critical without the proper restraints that the submarines systems offered or very slowly from radiation poisoning.

"The reactor is running normally, Sir."

"Thank God for that! OK, how are the batteries?" shouted Antipova.

"Batteries fully charged Sir."

"OK let's get ourselves back to base on battery power, we might just make it if we're lucky!"

"Aye, aye sir," replied the Helm, "we have propulsion, we have basic systems."

"Are we able to communicate with the satellite Helm?" asked Bartnev.

"No, Sir."

"Then get on the radio to base, tell them that we've had a major electronic storm across all our systems. Tell them we're limping home! Ask them to send us a tow!"

29) 17 October 2011, 21.00. Sat in the lounge of the villa.

Jorunn had made a delicious evening meal of vegetarian bangers and mash for everyone, and yet again Odd really enjoyed the meat free meal. After dinner Sam, Jenny, Svend and Freyer went to the snug lounge to have a long *get to know each other* chat. Spike went off to his bedroom to play on his gameboy in peace, Sarah was still catching up on her sleep so went to her bedroom and Odd decided to turn in too.

The lounge was large but snug with three large sofas placed around a huge wood burning stove that was throwing out a lot of heat.

"Heck, it's hot in here!" said Jenny taking her fleece off and throwing it over the back of one of the sofas, "Norway might be a cold country but the houses are really warm aren't they?"

"They are really warm, Jenny," agreed Freyer, "Norwegian houses are really well insulated, we've all got really warm homes, Norwegians don't like to be cold in their houses."

Jorunn brought in a jug of steaming hot cocoa and some chocolate cake and placed them down on the coffee table in front of the sofas.

"Hot chocolate everyone," she said cheerfully, "Enjoy! And now I'm going to bed too."

"Jorunn?" said Sam.

"Ja?"

"Can we get some pet chickens for our garden?"

"Pet chickens?"

"Yeah, I've always wanted some, then we can have the freshest of eggs every day, fresh eggs must be really nice, and I want to rescue the chickens."

"Rescue them?"

"Yeah, I want to get some chickens that have lived in those cramped little metal boxes all their lives, give them a good home. Can we Jorunn? Please! Can we?"

"Ja, I suppose so," she looked at Svend.

"Why not!" said Svend helping himself to some hot chocolate and a piece of cake, "we've got plenty of spare room. Go and speak to Alfie Blom tomorrow, he'll know where to get them and he'll build them a house too, or whatever you call the place where chickens live."

"It's a coop," said Jenny.

"Thanks, and Jorunn!" said Sam.

"Ja?"

"There are three old arm chairs in that store room next to my workshop, they look really old, a bit like rubbish really, they're just going to be thrown away. Could I have them for my experiments?"

"What kind of experiments?" she replied a little concerned.

"Oh, don't worry, just this and that." replied Sam.

Freyer smiled.

"What do you think, Freyer?" asked Jorunn.

"Oh, I suppose so, but don't make too much of a mess when you move them."

"I won't, I promise."

"Is that it?" asked Jorunn.

"Yes thank you," said Sam, "and thank you for looking after us today Jorunn."

Jorunn smiled.

After a few minutes Svend got up and went up to his bed, leaving just Sam, Jenny and Freyer sat in the lounge.

"Will you tell us about what happened to you and my Grandma, please Oldemor? asked Sam quietly. He was curious to know about his past.

"Will you tell us about what happened to the young women who couldn't run away first, please Freyer?" asked Jenny.

Freyer took a deep breath, "OK, OK. The history lesson first and then my own personal history lesson," smiled Freyer.

"Well you know I wasn't the only Norwegian girl to have fallen for a German boy during the war. They were all so charming you know, the Germans. They had lots of money, lots of food, and that was important because during the war many Norwegians didn't have much food at all. And there were no things like sweets and chocolate about, and not much fruit either. They were hard times, really hard. So when these soldiers came along, they were so friendly and they could give you lovely things, it was hard not to fall for them.

"How many girls like you were there?" asked Jenny.

"Oh, thousands I suppose, maybe ten thousand, maybe more, I don't know, lots of girls kept things a secret you know. It was their way of surviving.

"What happened to them if they stayed?" asked Sam.

"Well, they were called horrible names for one, they were spat at and people hit them."

"That must have been terrible," said Jenny.

"It must have been," agreed Freyer, "but worse was when the babies were born, they were taken away and put into orphanages."

"We're orphans," said Jenny, "well I am, Sam isn't any more."

"Sorry," said Sam.

"Don't be sorry Sam, I'm pleased for you, I really am."

"Thanks."

"But the orphanages back then were not like they are now. They were truly horrible places and lots of the people who worked in them weren't very nice to the children. The children were not treated like people they were treated like animals."

"I love animals," said Sam, "and I don't like the way that a lot of people treat them."

"I know Sam, well, when you grow up you can work to make the lives of animals as well as people better."

"I will" said Sam, "I will."

"So what happened to the children in these orphanages?" asked Jenny.

"They grew up Jenny, and when they did they were really confused as to why they'd been treated so badly when they'd done nothing wrong themselves. Many of them were really sick too. But most of them wanted answers. But do you know what the worst problem was?"

"No," said Jenny and Sam together.

"The worst problem was that some people tried to cover up what went on, they tried to say that certain things never happened, said it was all just a fantasy story."

"Why would they do that?" asked Sam.

"Have you heard of the ostrich syndrome, Sam?"

"No."

"I have," said Jenny.

"Tell Sam what it is then, Jenny."

"It where people bury their heads in the sand, they think that if they ignore something it will make it go away."

"Yeah that's right Jenny, they also think it will make something appear not to have happened. And in my experience, and I am very old and wise you know," Freyer smiled, "ignoring a problem doesn't make it go away, it often makes it worse!"

"So tell us what happened to you when you went to live in Sweden, Freyer?" said Jenny.

"Well, my life wasn't so bad I suppose, we had a nice house, plenty of money, a dog and a cat and a couple of horses, because I loved to ride, you know. I met a nice Swedish boy and we got married. He was very kind to me but we weren't blessed with children. Your Bestemor..."

"Bestemor?" asked Sam.

"Yes, that's the Norwegian word for grandmother, Sam."

"Oh."

"Anyway, your Bestemor, Agnes, was a very happy little girl who looked such a lot like you Sam, a girl though, not a boy," she chuckled.

"So how come you didn't know much about me Oldemor?"

"Oh, that was years and years later. Has anyone told you anything about your mother yet Sam?"

Sam shook his head "No, not yet, I don't even know her name, I know my father's name was Harald, but I don't know my mum's.

"Her name was Aesa, Sam."

"Aesa? That's a nice name."

"It means caring and intelligent."

"So how come you didn't know what happened to me Oldemor?"

"Well, it all happened such a long time ago Sam, people have arguments you know, then they blame people for things and refuse to speak, it's all very stupid.

"Adults are stupid," said Jenny, "it would be better if kids ran the world."

"Maybe," agreed Freyer, "anyway when Agnes died in a car crash Aesa was only twenty years old, it was just after she met your father, we were driving in a car one day, and I was driving. There was a terrible accident, I was quite badly hurt, Aesa was just scratched but Agnes was killed."

"Killed!" said Sam.

"Yes, it was terrible. But also, I didn't know it at the time, your mother, Aesa, was pregnant and because of the crash she lost the baby, it would have been your brother or sister.

"Brother or sister?"

"Yes, Sam. But when Agnes died it was just too much of a shock for your mother, too much for her to take in. And I suppose when Aesa lost the baby it pushed her over the edge. She started to hate me, she blamed me for the crash. I still do too, even to this very day. And I never spoke to her from that day on. I'd heard that there was another child, you, and that she'd given it away. But it was all so secret. I knew nothing more. So, Sam, that's where my story ends I suppose. I can't tell you why your parents sent you to England to be put into care. If I had been around I would have asked that you come and live with me, but I didn't know, I didn't know anything about you, she wouldn't speak with me you see."

30) 18 October 2011, 10.30. Alfie Blom

The weather had turned much more settled on the Sunday, and the islands were bathed in warm autumn sunshine and just light winds. Jenny and Spike had run down to breakfast, where they met Sam before going off the find the elusive Alfie Blom. They were told he lived over the cliffs in a small hut on his own beach a short distance away. They were told that he was an artist. Sam, Jenny and Spike sprinted out of the villa and headed in the direction where Jorunn had suggested.

"That was a sad story last night," said Jenny as they ran.

"Yeah," said Sam deep in thought. He couldn't sleep because of what Freyer had said, it just kept going through his mind about his mum not speaking to Oldemor. So, he'd got up well before dawn, grabbed some bread and jam from the kitchen and locked himself away in his workshop for a few hours to do some work on his rocket chairs. He'd managed to find the other three chairs in the store and had been really busy adapting them. He always found that he could think about things better while he tinkered around.

"What?" asked Spike.

"Never mind Spike, we'll tell you later." said Jenny.

"Where do you think this Alfie Blom man lives?" asked Spike.

"Dunno," said Sam, "Over there somewhere they said."

As they got to the dramatic cliff edge they could see that this morning the sea was still and calm.

"It's like a duck pond today," said Spike.

"Yeah," agreed Sam.

"Look! Down there!" pointed Jenny.

"Down to their left about half a mile away was a small, wooden cottage right on the beach. White smoke was puffing steadily out of its chimney.

"Someone's in!" said Jenny.

"Let's go and see if that's where Alfie Blom lives." said Sam.

The three made their way carefully down the steep cliff steps that led them on to the small cove. Outside the house were two big black dogs guarding the hut.

"Look!" shouted Sam, "Greyhounds!"

"Ja, Greyhounds!" the voice was right behind them, they spun round, startled, "not great guard dogs but they're good friends of mine!"

"Who are you?" gasped Sam.

"Who are *you*?" asked the man.

"We asked first!" said Jenny defensively.

"But I live here!" replied the man.

"But he's the new Chieftain!" said Spike pointing to Sam.

The old man grinned a big grin and stuck out a welcoming hand, "You must be Sam Marsh then?"

"Yes, but who are you?"

"Alfie Blom!"

"Oh, Mr Blom, we've been looking for you." said Sam.

"Have you? Why?"

"Chickens!" said Jenny.

"Chickens? Ah, chickens? You want some?"

"Yes please, but we want rescued birds Mr Blom," said Sam.

"Alfie, please call me Alfie, now come on down to my hut and have a drink of warm cloudberry juice why don't you, we can talk things through better in there."

Alfie Blom led them down the steps to his hut which was sat right at the top of the beach.

"Isn't it a bit dangerous having a hut right next to the sea?" asked Spike, "Won't it get washed away or something in the storms?"

"Well, it's been here for over fifty years young man and it hasn't been washed away yet!" laughed the old man.

Alfie Blom was an interesting but strange looking man. More like a cartoon character than a real person. He was dressed in a multicoloured suit, it was just as if someone had got a multi coloured paint pot and splashed it on his clothes. There were dashes of colour all over it but there was no pattern to it. He was wearing a huge black cowboy hat on his head and big cowboy boots on his feet. Everywhere around the hut were weird and wonderful sculptures.

"What are these, Alfie?" asked Sam as he looked at some strange totem pole things made out of drift wood. On one of the tall pieces of wood were carved the faces of people, some smiling, some scowling, birds, dogs, cats, and on top was the carving of a large ugly fishes head.

"They're my sculptures. Do you like that one?"

"Er, yeah I suppose I do," replied Sam, completely unsure about the object he was stood next to.

"It's a kind of totem pole, it's made from a piece of wood that washed up on this beach. I found it one day."

"Why is there a funny fishy head on the top?" asked Spike "it's an ugly fish head too."

Alfie laughed, "That's Kongetorsk or King Cod," he explained, "every now and again the fishermen would catch a fish with a strange deformed head, and they would keep the fish and hang it on a piece of string, it helped them forecast the weather, it was very important to the fishermen because the weather was very important to them. If they went out in weather that was too bad they could easily die."

"But why did you use it?" asked Jenny.

"I just liked the idea of putting Kongetorsk on top of my totem pole, I just make or paint things that I like the look of, why else would you do something?"

"Are you an artist then, Alfie?" asked Sam.

"Yes, can't you tell, all of these pieces of art scattered around!"

"Not really," said Jenny, "I thought it was just old junk!"

Alfie presented the three with a strange steaming hot orange coloured drink.

"What's this? asked Spike suspiciously.

"Cloudberry juice."

"What are cloudberries, I've never heard of them?" asked Sam.

"Cloudberries, Sam, are a bit like a bramble, a blackberry, but they tend to grow in mountainous or high areas. They don't mind the cold at all that's why they grow so well in Norway. But it does grow in Britain too you know."

"I've never heard of it!" said Jenny.

"Do you go out picking berries, Jenny?"

"Well no, not much," admitted Jenny.

"It tastes funny," said Spike pulling a face as he tried it.

"I think it tastes nice," said Sam.

"That's because you're Norwegian, Sam," said Alfie, "Norwegians love cloudberries!"

"You've got a lot of fish paintings and fish statues Alfie," said Jenny looking around the hut which was jam packed with paintings, drawings and models.

"Well fish and especially cod are really important to the Lofoten Islands."

"Are they?" she asked.

"Yes, for sure! For over one thousand years our small islands have been a world centre for cod fishing you know. Do any of you know when there are most cod in our waters?"

"The summer?" said Spike.

Alfie shook his head.

"The spring?" guessed Jenny.

"No."

"Autumn?" added Sam.

"All wrong!" said Alfie laughing, "It's winter! Winter is when there are the most cod in our waters because that's when these fish are migrating from the Barents Sea far to the north. Do you know what happens to the fish after they've been caught?"

"They die!" said Sam.

"Well yes they do, and that is a shame but I was thinking about how we preserve them."

"You freeze them?" suggested Jenny.

"Well, there weren't many freezers around a thousand years ago were there?"

"No, suppose not."

"We dry the fish. They are hung up on big racks and they hang out in the winter sun. The very cold wind blows through them all winter long and dries them right out. This dried fish is called Stockfish. For hundreds and hundreds of year we've sent the Stockfish all over the world, even today we send it to the four corners of the globe. It's very important for the economy not just of Lofoten but of all Norway you know."

"Where does the word Lofoten come from?" asked Sam curiously.

"Ah, that's a good question, Sam," said Alfie, "Lofoten is made up of hundreds of islands, some of them tiny, the island that we are on now is called Vågan. But originally Lofotr was the name for just one of the Lofoten Islands, the island of Vestvågøy, it was Lofotr, but later the name started to be used for all the islands."

"Do you know everything about the islands, Alfie?" asked Sam.

"Not everything," he laughed, "a lot, but not everything."

"I read you have a reef here?" said Jenny.

"Ja, we do have a reef, Jenny, which is actually the world's largest deep water coral reef! It's called the Røst Reef, because it's located west of Røst, and it's 40 km long you know."

"But the water must be cold here?" said Spike trying his hot cloudberry juice again, he still didn't like it much, he preferred Coke.

"Well, the water is cold but not as cold as you would think because of something called the gulf stream. Do you know what that is anyone?"

This was turning out to be like a day at school except that the classroom was a bit more interesting than the ones back in Holmford.

"It's like a special strong, warm wind that flows all the way from Mexico, I think, and nearly all the way to the North Pole," explained Sam, "I think it goes over Britain too."

"It does Sam, for most of the year it does."

"But how can a wind make the water warm?" asked Spike.

"Well, the wind makes weather systems and these drag warm waters along with them too, that's how," explained Alfie.

Everyone was silent for a few minutes.

"Alfie?" said Sam, he'd had enough of history and geography lessons for one morning.

"Ja?"

"Do you know where we can get some rescue chickens from?"

"Ah, yes, that was why you came to find me, wasn't it?"

"Yes."

"Well yes, I have a friend that can get you some if you like, he rescues them from battery farms over on the mainland then sells them to people that want chickens of their own."

"Do they lay eggs alright after being in one of those places, though?" asked Spike, "aren't they tired out or something?"

"Ja, for sure, they are tired, but after a bit of pecking on some nice grass they get better. There's no problems with egg laying, they don't lay every day but they still have a lot to offer. How many do you want, Sam?"

"Er dunno, about fifty!"

"Fifty is a lot of chickens, you know."

"Yeah I know, but you just said that they won't all lay every day."

"I can get you a big coop for them too if you like."

"Thanks."

"Well we'd better be getting off home Alfie," said Sam.

"Do you want to go and see the reef?" asked Alfie.

"The reef?" replied Sam.

"Ja the Røst Reef, do you want to go and see it tomorrow morning? Are you here for a long visit Jenny and Spike?"

"Just the week, it's the half term holidays."

"OK, well would you like to come? I've got a mini sub you know."

"A mini sub?" gulped Spike, "Yeah, count me in."

"OK," agreed Jenny

"Great," said Sam.

"Then until tomorrow morning at 9 o'clock. The weather forecast is good, look, Kongetorsk says it's going to be good tomorrow morning! After that, tomorrow evening, he says there will be a bad storm! He is always right!"

31) 19 October 2011, 8.00 am. Diving with Alfie Blom.

Kongetorsk was right about the weather, Monday was a beautiful day, perhaps even sunnier than the day before, and the forecast for most of the day was for calm, clear seas, but they warned that there was a very big storm heading for the islands in the late afternoon which could last for a few days.

"You will both be going with them won't you?" asked Freyer to Odd and Svend.

"I'll be going," said Svend, "Odd here is not the world's best sailor," Svend nudged Odd playfully, "he get's sea sick."

"No he's right, I do. I hate the sea! Me and the sea don't go together at all, but thankfully Svend here was brought up by a sailor, he loves the ocean, he's a very experienced sailor."

"Yes I am, my dad was an Admiral, he taught me to sail a dinghy when I was four years old, I even sailed round the world when I was a student."

"On your own?"

"No, no there was a crew of us, but it was still a fantastic challenge. No, don't worry, Freyer, I understand that Alfie was a submariner for many years, and he's authorised to look after Sam, he's very highly qualified to pilot his DSV around the reef, he sometimes takes tourists around, you know."

"How big's this DSV thing?"

"Yeah, Deep Submersival Vehicle, oh, it's only small, it can carry a maximum of five people. But I'm not going down with them, I'll stay on board the ship, we'll take out a small crew of sailors, they stay with the royal ship all the time. Don't worry they'll be fine and they'll have a great time. How many kids get to go out in a private DSV and snoop around a coral reef?"

"Not too many I suppose."

"Oh, here they are now!"

"Hi Svend, Hi Odd, Jorunn, morning Oldemor."

"Hello darling, did you sleep well?"

"Yeah great, thanks."

"What's for breakfast?" muttered Spike.

"It's all on the breakfast bar Spike!" called Jorunn.

"I think I'll just have some fruit and a juice," said Jenny.

"Jenny's the healthy one!" mumbled Spike as he piled his plate up with goodies, "me, I'm the pig!"

"That's true!" added Jenny.

"Are you looking forward to going out in the submarine, Sam?" asked Freyer.

"Yeah!" said Sam.

The phone in the hall started ringing.

"I'll get it." said Odd

He went and answered the phone, then he called for Sarah, "Sarah, phone for you, it's England!"

Sarah came down quickly from her room and spoke on the phone for a few minutes before coming into the kitchen looking a little flustered.

"That was my office,"

"What's the matter, Sarah?" asked Freyer.

"They've got a big problem back home, it's all hands to the pumps I'm afraid, an emergency of some kind, they've been in touch with the Norwegian government and they have cleared it with them for me to go home for a couple of weeks."

"Oh!" said Sam, he really liked having Sarah around, she was his friend, and even though he kept on meeting lots of new people I was nice have a familiar face around.

"Don't worry Sam," said Sarah, "I'll be back, I have to come back, it's the law, until you are made a Norwegian citizen I have to stay, and I don't know how long that will take," she looked at Svend. "Do you know Svend?"

"I think it could take months Sarah, but I'm not exactly sure."

"When do you have to go?" asked Jenny.

"This morning."

"On the Aerion?" asked Spike excitedly.

"No such luck," replied Sarah, I have to fly from Svolvaer to Bergen and then take an afternoon flight from Bergen to Leeds Airport. So I'd better get packing. Can someone take me to the airport?"

"I can," said Odd, "Svend's going diving with the kids and Alfie this morning, I don't like the sea so I'm not, so I can take you just as soon as you're ready.

"Well," said Svend looking at his watch, "we should be going now, we're meeting Alfie at his jetty, then our royal boat has to go and collect the DSV from Svolvaer, we've got a lot to do, we'd better get going."

Svend, Sam, Jenny and Spike made their way through the large grounds of the villa and down the cliffs to the right of where they'd been the day before. Just as they climbed down the last flight of cliff steps the boat came into view for the first time.

"Wowee!" said Spike.

"Wow!" agreed Sam.

"Nice boat," said Jenny completely unphased.

"When you said boat, Svend," said Sam, "I thought it would be some kind of fancy fishing boat or a funny yacht or something, I never thought it would be a battle ship!"

"Well it's not exactly a battleship, Sam."

"But it's got guns!" said Spike.

"It's not a battleship," continued Svend, "but it is a Norwegian Navy ship."

"What is it then?" asked Spike before Sam could ask the same question.

"It's a Super Hauk class patrol boat, they were designed by a man called Captain Harald Henriksen. Norway has 14 of these Super Hauk class vessels and they make up the Coastal Combat flotilla, which is responsible for protecting our beautiful but very long Norwegian coastline."

"What? They just sail up and down the coast all day?" asked Spike.

"Just sailing up and down the coast Spike is a very important job, Norway is a very long country and we have a lot of coastline."

"How much?" asked Sam.

"Over 25 thousand kilometres, Sam, because that includes all our beautiful fjords."

"So it is a very big job!" sneered Jenny at Spike and Sam.

"Yes, very big."

"But today and every day this Super Hauk is ours?" asked Sam.

"This Super Hauk is called Skarv and she has been allocated to protect you and these islands by the government."

"Wicked!" said Sam.

As they walked toward the Skarv the sailors all stood to attention and saluted.

"Look, they're saluting you, Svend," chuckled Sam.

"They're not saluting me, Sam, they're saluting you, your parents were very highly regarded, they are giving you the same honour!"

"Thanks," said Sam to the sailors as he passed them, he didn't know what else to say.

"Thanks! Is that all you can say to them?" chuckled Spike nudging Sam "Thanks!"

"Well, what am I supposed to say?"

"I don't know, I'm not considered royalty! What's he supposed to say, Svend?"

"Er, at ease, I think."

"At ease!" called Sam and the sailors relaxed.

"Come on, let's go and have a word with the captain before we go and collect Alfie and then the DSV."

"Sam, this is Captain Vegar, he's in charge of the Skarv and responsible for patrolling the waters around our islands."

"Hi, Captain Vegar."

"Hello Sam, I understand Alfie Blom is taking you and your friends diving down to the reef in a DSV today."

"Yes, he is."

"Well, we need to make sure that we are all safely back on land by 1400 hours this afternoon because a big storm is due to hit our coast later."

"Oh, yeah, I knew about that, but are we safe to go diving this morning?"

"Ja, sure, it's calm for now, the conditions are good."

The Skarv was freed from her mooring and motored gently around the cliffs towards Alfie Blom's house which was just a couple of minutes sail.

"There he is!" called Jenny "there's Alfie!"

"Hi, Alfie!" called Sam and Spike.

"Hi, guys!"

Skarv pulled alongside his jetty and Alfie expertly hopped aboard without the help of the sailor.

"Ready for a spot of diving are we?" he asked. Today he was wearing a bright multi coloured fleece and pants, but he was wearing a sailor's cap instead of his Stetson and deck shoes instead of cowboy boots.

"Yeah!" said Sam, "is it far to the Røst Reef, Alfie?"

"No, not too far, this boat is very fast so once we've loaded up the DSV then it will take us about one hour to get over to the reef."

"How long will we dive for?" asked Jenny.

"Er, let me think," said Alfie, "we have to be back at port by 1400 hours because of the storm, so I think we can have about two hours to explore the reef, I think that is a good amount of time.

Soon after leaving Alfie Blom's jetty, Skarv was round at Svolvaer port and loading up the DSV which was carefully placed on the back of the ship by a special crane.

"She is very heavy!" called Captain Vegar, "but we can manage her! We have lots of power!"

Even fully loaded with the heavy DSV, Skarv still managed a quick 30 knots on her way to the reef. When directly above the Røst Reef she used a special winch to lower the mini sub down over the back and gently placed it in the water.

"Quick!" called Alfie who had jumped onto the sub as soon as it was in the water, "Come on! Let's go!" He was unhooking the cables.

"What?" said Spike warily.

"Come on, jump on!" called Alfie.

"What? Do you mean there's no ramp or anything?"

"No, we just jump on!"

"I'm not jumping over there, I might fall in!"

"You won't, it's safe!"

"I'm not jumping, actually I'm not all that bothered about going!"

Quickly without even thinking Jenny and Sam leapt the couple of feet over onto the DSV and started climbing down through the open hatch into the bubble that they would sit in.

"Come on, Spike, it's easy!" called Sam before his head disappeared down below.

"No, no, I'm alright, I think I'm going to stay up here, they might need a hand with something. I'd better stay."

"They won't need a hand with anything, Spike! They're sailors!" called Jenny, "you're just a scared kid!"

"No, no I'm not, I'm not scared," gulped Spike, "It's just I don't think there's enough room for four people on that, that thing. It's tiny!"

"There's plenty of room Spike!" called Alfie laughing, "but if you want to stay over there, it's no problem."

"Yeah, I think I will stay," said Spike quietly.

A young sailor pushed the DSV away from the boat and Alfie fired up the motors.

"Don't worry, Spike," said Svend putting his arm around Spike, "we can watch everything they do from the control room, come on, we won't miss a thing!"

Inside the cramped DSV Alfie was at the controls, which looked like the cockpit of a plane. "Are you two ready?" he asked.

"Yeah," said Sam, "I'm sorry about Spike, I thought he wanted to come."

"No worries, sometimes submarines have that effect on people, they like the idea of them until they have to get inside one and actually go under the water. OK, if we're all ready let's dive!"

The DSV started sinking into the depths of the North Sea which was quite clear because the waters were so calm. The odd seal and dolphin came to investigate as they went deeper and deeper.

"You know," said Alfie, "that this reef was only discovered in the year 2002."

"Was it?" said Jenny.

"Yeah, it forms a chain of deep sea cold water reefs that stretch all the way from here right around Europe to North Africa. But in Norway we have just for ourselves two thousand square kilometres of reef."

The water was a bit murky as they got down to the reef. But they could still see the coral clearly and all the different kinds of fish and other sea creatures that lived on it.

"It's a living creature you know," said Alfie.

"What is?" said Jenny.

"The reef itself, it's a living creature. The corals are alive, it's always growing, bits dying, others being born, I suppose, all the time. Scientists think that we have just six kinds of coral here in Norway, but in some warm water reefs they have hundreds of different kinds of coral. Because these waters are much colder than the water around a warm reef, like the Great Barrier Reef in Australia, it tends to grow much more slowly. In fact some scientists have proved that even the fish down here live longer than in warmer parts of the world."

"Have you been to the Great Barrier Reef, Alfie?" asked Sam.

"Ja, years ago I went, I actually dived on it a few times, it was amazing, so huge, but this reef is really fantastic too. It's so full of life. It is amazing. It is really important for the ecosystem of the ocean. It's like one big chain you see."

"What do you mean, Alfie?" asked Jenny.

"The reef has lots of this stuff called suspended organic matter and zooplankton, it's tiny stuff that you need a microscope to see. It's all around the reef and that's what feeds the coral and all the small fish. These small fish are food for larger fish and the larger fish are food for sea birds, seals, dolphins and killer whales, it's like a chain, everything is connected, every part is important.

"Do we really have Orca's here too?" asked Sam.

"Ja! We have the best Orca's in the world in Norway, Sam. We also get big sharks like Basking Sharks visiting us. Now, *they* are a big fish!"

The DSV spent over an hour touring around the reef, watching all the different forms of sea life and corals.

But on their way back to the ship they spotted something unusual, part of the reef looked different.

"What's that there, Alfie?" said Sam pointing.

"I don't know, where?"

"There!"

"Oh, I see. It looks like a stretch of dead reef, but it's quite a large piece, reef doesn't normally do that, it's constantly regenerating itself. That only happens when there's a problem, a disease or some kind of contamination."

"There's a lot of dead reef there though, Alfie," added Jenny.

"Ja, there is, let's go and take a closer look, I'll just speak with the control room first. Svend, are you there?"

"I'm here Alfie, go ahead."

"Can you see the dead part of the reef up there, Svend?"

"Yeah we can see it, it looks strange."

"We're going in to take a closer look, I'm going to use the robotic arms to take some samples from the coral, we can send it to the lab in Bergen to be analysed."

"Good idea, but be careful."

"Ja, no problem, careful is my middle name!"

Alfie took the DSV close into the reef and the contamination looked terrible up close. It went on for about one hundred and fifty metres. Lots of the coral had been broken, smashed and ripped apart. Suddenly, there was something visible below the reef.

"What's that?" said Jenny.

"What?" said Alfie.

"There! Look! Down there!"

Well hidden, right underneath a ridge of coral was something metal, a large metal shape, long and smooth.

"I don't know," said Alfie, "I'm going in for a look."

"It's a ship," said Sam.

"Er, no, I don't think so," said Alfie, "It's something though, no, it's a submarine, but it's been here for years. Look! All the reef has grown over it, it's almost a part of the reef. It must have been here over fifty years for that level of growth, but someone has been here recently, they've destroyed part of the reef to get to it. I wonder why?"

"I can see a name," said Sam.

"Yeah, so can I," agreed Jenny, "Helmsfjord, it says Helmsfjord," Jenny got a cheap disposable camera out of her pocket and started snapping the Helmsfjord eagerly.

"Helmsfjord? I've heard of that, don't know where from but I've definitely heard of it."

"Maybe Svend will know?" said Sam.

"Svend, have you heard of a submarine called the Helmsfjord?" asked Alfie.

"No, don't think so, but I'll take a look on the Navy database, I've got access from here, just a minute..wait, that's funny, there is something here but I can't access the information. I have high level clearance, so I should be able to see this file but it's not letting me. You'd better come back up, take some pictures and make a note of the exact co-ordinates and then come straight up."

32) 19 October 2011, 12 noon. Bridge of the Unterwasserwelt.

"Herr Krater our sensors have detected some activity over the wreck of the Helmsfjord," reported Commander Reich from the bridge of the Unterwasserwelt.

"What kind of activity Herr Reich? Sea mammals?"

"No, Sir, a mini sub of some kind, maybe a DSV, I can't be sure, the coral is distorting our sensors."

"Coral is disturbing your sensors?" replied Krater, "a few bits of rock shouldn't interfere with the most advanced technology in the world, Reich!"

"Coral is not rock sir and I think that's the problem."

"What are they actually doing now, can you see that?"

"I think they're going back to the surface. But I cannot be certain whether they went close enough to make a positive identification of the Helmsfjord, Sir."

"You will have to do something about it, Reich. Destroy the stray!"

"Destroy it! But I can't do that!"

"You do not tell me what to do Commander Reich!" Krater was furious, "I give the orders around here!"

"Sorry, Sir, but with respect if we destroy that sub then we will arouse suspicion, then there will be a search, an enquiry, an investigation. More boats, more subs and divers will arrive and then we will have blown everything. Sir, I strongly suggest that we do nothing to make the situation worse."

"Nothing?"

"Precisely."

"To do nothing is not an option Reich, I've have not got where I am today doing nothing! We have to do something. I suspect we have already aroused their suspicions, Commander, we must try and destroy any evidence they have, that will at least give us some time to play with."

"What do you suggest, Sir?"

"Scramble their electronic systems, if I am correct, scrambling them will erase any information they have recorded whilst diving."

"That's correct, Sir. But if they have an umbilical connection to a ship then the information may well be stored on the ship's computers too."

"Scramble them both!"

"I can't, Sir, I can't scramble a surface ship from this distance and the X boats are too far away to do it either. I fear we may have to scramble the sub and hope for the best."

"Hope for the best?" Krater was furious and about to explode.

"Yes, Sir. We have no other option that will not arouse any interest in our project. I'm sure they have very little information and with the storm approaching and due to remain for three or four days that may give us the time we need to board the Helmsford and get the safe out. Our robodivers are ready to get in there at a moment's notice when we get there."

Krater calmed down and thought for a moment, "Very well, Reich, I agree with your thinking, we can't take any risks not this close to getting the information, we can't arouse suspicion, scramble the sub and leave the boat alone. Get on with it."

33) 19 October 2011, 12.05. On board the DSV.

As the DSV rose steadily to the surface suddenly things started to go badly wrong. Suddenly all the power cut off and inside the sub and it went very dark even though they were quite close to the surface. Almost straight away the auxiliary power kicked in and a dim light came on in the cockpit.

"What's happened?" asked a worried Jenny.

"I don't know," said Alfie, "the main power has all gone and all the controls have stopped working."

"Why would that happen?" asked Sam.

"I don't know, it's never happened before."

"Can we speak with the surface?" asked Sam.

"No, the comms link has gone down too. It shouldn't be a major problem though, they know we're on the way up and they knew our last co-ordinates. They've got sonar so they can ping us. We will be OK, don't worry.

The mini sub rose gently up to the surface and discovered they were still about two hundred metres from the Skarv. The boat seemed to see them rise to the surface and quickly turned to come towards them. When the Skarv was right next to the sub, the sailors threw lines over and then connected the clips to start hauling it on board. Svend was the first on the roof of the DSV opening the hatch.

"What just happened?" he shouted down, "Is everyone OK?"

"Ja fine! Don't know what happened though," replied Alfie, "all the power just went down and all the systems failed. I've tried rebooting everything but we've got nothing, everything is offline. The computer systems seem to have gone completely gaga!"

"Are you kids alright?" Svend called out.

"Yeah, we're fine!" replied Sam.

"We'd like to get out though," added Jenny.

"Come on up then!"

Jenny climbed out of the sub and was glad to be breathing fresh air again. A worried looking Spike was stood looking at the DSV.

"What happened down there?" he asked.

"Dunno," said Sam as he climbed down off the sub, "one second we were rising steadily to the surface and the next we had no power, no systems, nothing, it all just went off."

"Maybe some kind of virus?" said Spike, "I can take a look at the on board computer if you like."

"No, that's alright," said Alfie, "we'll leave that to the technicians."

"No, Spike's a genius with computers Alfie, he probably knows more than the technicians," said Jenny.

Alfie looked at Sam

"She's right, he's a wizard with computers, let him have a look."

"Alright then," agreed Alfie, "come on board Spike, see what you think."

Spike climbed on board the sub and down into the cabin whilst the crew of the Skarv secured it to the deck before they set off back towards Svolvaer.

After fifteen minutes Spike hauled himself out of the DSV and joined the rest of the team in the lounge, where they were having some sandwiches and hot chocolate to drink.

"Did you find anything Spike?" asked Alfie.

Spike had a very worried look on his face.

"What's the matter Spike, what is it?" asked Sam.

"Well, I've been through everything I can, all the systems, which are really quite simple, it was no challenge at all really."

"Spike!" prompted Jenny, "just tell us what you discovered."

"Alright, well all the systems crashed because somebody made them crash!"

"What?" said Svend, "Somebody made them crash, who?"

"I don't know that."

"Tell us why you think that please, Spike?" said Alfie calmly, "Do you have any proof?"

"It's clear as the nose on your face what's happened, someone's scrambled you!"

Everyone was quiet for a while.

"Sorry Spike, you lost me for one," said Svend "What's scrambling?"

"Scrambling is when somebody uses a signal to break up something else, you can break up a telephone call by scrambling it."

"But can't you unscramble a telephone call too?" said Jenny.

"Yeah, easy, you just need to know what frequency it's being scrambled on, it's sort of like a code, if you know the code you can unpick a scramble."

"Somebody deliberately scrambled up our systems and that caused everything to go offline, power, computer, everything?" asked Alfie.

"Yep."

"Who?"

"Don't know but when I get back to the villa I could use the laptop in my room to trace it."

"You can?" said Svend.

"Sure!"

"But you can't tell us who it was?"

"I can tell you what sort of computer system it was and that may be able to help us identify who did it, that's all I can do."

34) 19 October 2011, 14.30. Bad Atlantic storm.

It was 2.30 when the team arrived back at the villa and the weather was just starting to close in on the islands. Alfie had gone to collect his dogs before coming up to the villa with them, he said they didn't like storms, it upset them. But by the time they'd all walked up to the villa from the royal jetty there was a knock on the door and Alfie and his dogs were there.

"Can the dog's come in?" he called.

"Yeah!" said Sam who started making a fuss of them as they wagged their tails furiously.

"They'll settle down in front of the wood burner in a minute," said Alfie, "they're really no bother."

"Wipe their feet, Alfie!" shouted Jorunn from the kitchen.

"OK Jorunn!" he replied, then he turned to Sam "don't ever argue with Jorunn, Sam, she's a crazy woman when she's angry, and she's got a big rolling pin! Oh, who's this?"

Freyer had just appeared and was also making a fuss of the dogs.

"Oh yeah, Alfie this is my Great Grandma Freyer, Freyer, this is Alfie Blom."

"Hi Alfie Blom!"

"Hello Oldemor! Nice to meet you."

"And you."

"Are you lot coming up or what!" called Spike from his room, "I think I might have something interesting."

Alfie, Freyer and Sam rushed up to Spike's room only to discover Svend and Jenny were already there, the dogs followed them up and jumped straight on the bed. Alfie looked at Sam, then at Freyer, then at Spike.

"They're OK on the bed," said Spike, "just shift them if Jorunn comes up. Now look at this!"

On the screen of Spike's laptop were loads of weird looking figures, co-ordinates and numbers which didn't seem to make sense to anyone apart from Spike, Alfie and Svend.

"Daddah!" said Spike really pleased with himself, both his hands were directed towards the computer. Alfie and Svend were staring at each other, they had worried looks on their faces.

"What is it?" said Sam.

"What does all that mean?" asked Jenny.

"You tell them, Spike," said Svend.

"OK, I've traced that scrambling signal, it wasn't hidden very well at all, whoever did it was so sure of themselves they never thought in a month of Sundays that anyone would even think of tracing them, thought that no-one would imagine that there was anyone there."

"Where?" said Freyer.

"At the bottom of the ocean!"

"What? A submarine scrambled our mini sub?" asked Jenny.

"Not any submarine I've ever heard of!" added Alfie.

"What then?" said Sam.

"Well I've done a trace on the scale of the sender, I can see what level of power would be needed to send that sort of signal."

"You can do that?" said Freyer impressed.

"Already have, Freyer, already have," Spike loved computers, "and whatever scrambled you this afternoon was massive, completely massive, it cannot be a submarine, it's got more power even than a Nimitz class aircraft carrier could generate.

It has to be some kind of undersea military base. A *massive* undersea military base!"

"I don't know of any underwater bases!" said Alfie.

"Me neither," mumbled Svend.

"What can it be then?" asked Jenny.

"I don't know, but I do know that the scrambling signal was sent just after you discovered that old wreck under the reef. The timings are very exact," said Spike.

"You can work that out?" asked Sam.

"Yeah, we were watching and recording everything you were doing, we saw that wreck too, remember you asked Svend to look it up."

"Oh, yeah," said Sam.

"Whoever blew your subs systems did not want you making information about that wreck public knowledge."

"I wonder what's on the Helmsfjord sub?" said Sam.

35) 19 October 2011, 16.30. Unterwasserwelt arrives.

On the surface of the sea the storm was blowing to galeforce, all flights into and out of Svolvaer airport had been suspended because it was proving dangerous for planes to land or take off safely. Thankfully, Sarah would have been almost at Leeds Airport by the time the storm hit land. But Odd, who had been running some errands in town was caught up in the torrential downpour and 70 miles per hour winds as he slowly made his way back to the villa in the Range Rover.

But deep on the ocean floor Unterwasserwelt was unaffected by the stormy conditions on the surface. Close to the top of the reef the waves were strong, but where she was sat on the ocean floor, over 150 metres further down, it was quiet. Down this deep there was just darkness.

Commander Reich had insisted that The Company hired a small group of submariners that he had worked with for years. Men he could trust completely. They'd all been security screened and were all offered massive salaries and golden 'hellos' from Krater. For the moment Reich's second in command, Executive Officer, Alfred Schmidt was in charge of the vast undersea base.

"We have reached our destination point, Sir," said the robot that was at the helm.

"All stop!" replied Schmidt.

"All stop, Sir," replied the robot.

"Summon Commander Reich to the bridge."

"Aye, aye Sir."

Three minutes later Reich appeared on the bridge.

"Status, Number One?" he asked

"We have arrived at our destination, Sir," replied Schmit.

"What's the water depth here, Ally?"

"One hundred and eighty five metres, Sir."

"Good, nice and deep, well away from any prying eyes, eh?"

"Ja, Sir."

"Summon Herr Krater on the video link Communications Robot."

"Aye, aye Sir," replied the Communications Robot. After forty five seconds he spoke again, "I have Herr Krater on the link, Sir."

"Herr Krater, good news, we have reached our destination, Sir."

"What is your current depth and position, Reich?"

"We are at one hundred and eighty five metres, and we are approximately four kilometres from the target."

"Excellent, and the visitors, have you heard any more from them Commander?"

"No Sir, all is quiet, their systems were scrambled but they floated to the surface and then departed almost instantly."

"And nothing since?"

"No Sir, all quiet."

"Excellent work Reich."

"What are my instructions now Sir?

"Send out the Robodivers to take a look at the submarine, I want their report on my desk when I arrive with you in approximately two hours."

"Aye Sir, Reich out."

Reich immediately turned to his XO.

"Order the Robodivers to attend the wreck, make a full reconnaissance of its position, how it lies in the water, access possibilities, etc."

"Do you want them to open her up and investigate the interior, Sir?"

"No, not yet, Herr Krater thinks that the wreck will be potentially unstable, he does not want to risk any damage to the safe."

"Is the safe watertight Sir?"

"Yes, Herr Krater placed the documents in the safe himself, it was he who closed the vault and he states that it is completely water tight."

Within five minutes the two immense Robodivers were getting into the torpedo tubes and getting ready to be blasted out. The Robodivers were much larger than the other androids which were a standard two metres tall and a normal humanoid shape. In contrast to this Robodivers were very tall, very sleek creations. Three metres tall but extremely skinny to fit inside the 533 millimetre torpedo tubes, their thin shape made them perfectly streamlined for moving through the water quickly.

In charge of the torpedo room was Gurt Zimmermann, a forty five year old submarine veteran. This new Unterwasserwelt had revitalised his flagging career. He was about to leave the navy after twenty seven years until his good friend Dirk Reich had called him up when he was on shore leave. He'd said he was leaving the navy for a commercial project. A top secret new venture where the money and opportunities were just too good to miss. If he came to work for him he said, he would be given a five year contract then he could retire to a beach side apartment in the Canary Islands. With two ex-wives to keep happy and seven kids it was an offer just too good to ignore for Zimmermann, the man that Dirk Reich considered to be one of the best torpedo technicians on the planet.

"Robodivers are you ready?" asked Zimmermann, he could never quite get over the fact that they weren't people. He always wanted to chat with them. But they never responded.

"Aye, Sir!" said Robodiver number one.

"Aye, Sir!" said number two.

"Prepare for launch!"

Zimmermann closed the tubes personally, he didn't trust a robot to do something that could affect him, could even kill him if it wasn't done properly.

He started the countdown, "Three, two, one, number one tube away, three, two, one, number two tube away."

Torpedoes are self propelled underwater missiles that are fired out of a variety of craft, helicopters, surface ships, even from the land, but they are most effective when fired from submarines. They are fired out of compressed air tubes. Once fired the Robodivers swam towards to the site of the Helmsfjord at over sixty knots.

Back on the bridge, Robodiver number one was already reporting his initial findings to Commander Reich.

"Outer casing of the target very badly deteriorated Sir. The Reef has enveloped the hull. Large hole in the side."

"Proceed to the vicinity of the safe. What is its condition?"

"Target area is under the reef, Sir."

"Can you break the reef and make contact with the hull to scan it, number two?"

"Making contact with reef now, removing coral, contact made with target area of hull, scanning now, connecting the results with the bridge sir."

On a big screen on the bridge Robodiver number two's scan was clearly visible.

"There it is!" called the XO.

"Where?" replied Reich.

"Go back!"

"Go back number two, slowly, back five percent."

"Aye Sir!"

The scan slowly retraced its steps.

"Stop!" called Schmidt.

"Aye, Sir," responded number two from the hull of the Helmsfjord.

"There it is sir, that's the safe, I'm sure of it."

"I see it now."

"Robodiver number one, scan the safe, assess whether it has been corrupted by water."

"Aye, Sir...scan complete, safe has not been corrupted by the sea, it is watertight, Sir."

"Excellent news!" smiled Reich, "Number one, take a GPS reading of the safe and then return to base."

"Aye, Sir."

"Tomorrow morning," said Reich to Schmidt, "we will enter the Helmsfjord and bring the safe back to Unterwasserwelt, the future is in our hands, old friend."

36) 19 October 2011, 20.00 hours. Royal villa.

Outside it was pitch black and the terrible storm was raging, beating and battering the islands. No one dared venture outside in case they were blown over the cliffs, the storm was so fierce and the winds so strong.

Sam, Spike, Alfie, Svend and Odd were pouring over the information that Spike had discovered. Jenny and Freyer had disappeared downstairs to watch English satellite television. Svend had reported his findings to his superiors but they hadn't seemed interested in what they'd discovered whilst on the reef. Even when Svend told them about the scrambling, a terrible security breech, they weren't interested. Alfie had been stewing over this lack of enthusiasm for over an hour now and suddenly exploded to life.

"This is really bad, this is really serious, there's something down there, I'm sure of it, and it's got something to do with that wreck under the reef. This is not a normal situation at all. I don't like it. I'm going to call an old friend, me and him go back years and years."

Alfie got his mobile out and stared at his watch for a few seconds. It was if he was trying to work something out. He selected a speed dial number.

"Rear Admiral Alfie Blom, Svolvaer for the National Security Advisor," he said formally.

Svend and Odd stared at each other in complete disbelief,

"Rear Admiral?" whispered Svend to his colleague.

"God Dag to you too Slim," said Alfie after a twenty second wait, " how is life in DC? Good. How're Martha and the little ones?...I've sold a few, I'll have you know that I have a very exclusive market for my work, hahaha, it's highly sought after! King Cod? You like it? I'll send it over for Christmas then, a present, yeah it'll look mighty impressive in your office, at least you'll be able to forecast the weather! Hahahaha!..Oh, yeah, right, no it's business not pleasure. We've got something to report. Yes, this line is secure Slim, no problems, you know me! Anyway, we were diving off the reef this morning, yeah the Røst Reef, and we discovered a wreck, no, no that's nothing unusual, there are quite a few scattered about down there, it's what happened next that will interest you. When we were going back to the surface we were scrambled, no, no I'm not *exactly* sure of what happened but I have a young man next to me, a whizz kid he is, you'll like him Slim, no he's English, he discovered it was a scramble and he's traced it. Just a minute Slim I'll put him on." Alfie passed the phone to Spike who didn't know what to do because he didn't have a clue who he was speaking to, "Will you just explain everything you know to my friend Slim, Spike, don't worry there's no rights or wrongs, just tell him what you think is going on, please. Here I'll put it on speaker phone if you like. Slim I'm putting you on to speakerphone!"

"OK," said a smooth American voice over the answerphone.

"Hi," said Spike.

"Spike?"

"Yeah,"

"Hi Spike, my name is Slim Easton, I'm the National Security Advisor here in Washington DC."

"America?"

"Yup, the very same. The good old US of A! Anyway Spike, I understand you traced a scramble this afternoon, can you tell me what you discovered?"

"Oh, yeah, no probs. Well, as Alfie told you, when Alfie and my friends Sam and Jenny were coming up in the DSV, all their power blew..."

"All their power?"

"Yeah, and their systems as well."

"Did they try and reboot the systems do you know?"

"Yes, we did," interrupted Alfie.

"And nothing?"

"No, nothing."

"Then what Spike?"

"Well, when the sub was dragged onto the ship I went on board and investigated the situation and I found that it had been scrambled by some kind of external device."

"So you know about these things son?"

"Yeah, quite a bit. Anyway, I took out the cpu..."

"You did?" asked a horrified Alfie, "I didn't know you did that!"

"Oh sorry," said Spike sheepishly.

"Let him go on, Alfie!" said Slim impatiently, "I gotta meeting with the chief inside ten, you know, you were lucky, you just caught me."

Alfie nodded to Spike, who continued, "So I connected up the cpu to my kit..."

"Your kit?" asked Slim.

"Yeah, I developed it myself, it's like my box of magic tricks. Then I connected my kit to the laptop and analysed the CPU, I discovered almost immediately that it had been scrambled. But the scramble, although very powerful, was quite simple, bog standard it was."

"Bog standard? What does that mean."

"Really, really simple, like a baby's toy!" explained Spike.

"Oh, OK, go on."

"Well, it was easy, I could pick it up straight away, and it only took me a few minutes to trace it. I traced its origin, the type of signal and its strength."

"Clever boy!" said Slim, "Can you send me that data straight away?"

"Yeah, no problem, what's your email address?"

"No! No emails, Spike, email isn't secure, give me your computer details and I'll bring you in."

Spike gave Slim all the details of the laptop he was working on, its serial number and model and within thirty seconds Slim had traced it and found him.

"I got you Spike, can you see me?"

On Spike's laptop had appeared a video link. There was a man's face staring at them.

"Not too multicoloured today I see, Alfie?" joked Slim.

"A bit dull today I'm afraid."

"OK, is that the information I can see in that open window?" Amazingly Slim had access to everything on Spike's computer.

"Yeah, it is."

"Give me two minute guys, I'm gonna put you all on hold, but don't touch anything I'll be straight back."

All was quiet in Spike's bedroom.

"Is that really the National Security Advisor to the American President?" asked Svend.

"Ja, it sure is," replied Alfie.

"And you are a Rear Admiral?" asked Sam.

"Ja!"

"We knew you were in the navy," said Odd, "but we thought you were just a retired submarine officer."

"I am a retired submarine officer, Odd, that's true, but I didn't spend all my career in subs, I did other things."

"Like what?" asked Spike.

"I can't tell you Spike, it's top secret."

Everyone thought Alfie was joking, but from the look on his face he wasn't.

"Hi y'all!" said Slim reappearing on the computer screen, "sorry about that, I just had to check out the information that you gave me."

"And what do you think, Slim?" asked Alfie.

"I think we got ourselves one heck of a big problem."

"What kind of a problem?"

"I think we got ourselves some kind of maniac sitting at the bottom of the ocean in one heck of big underwater vessel, taking pot shots at any passing sub or ship."

"Someone is down there?" said Sam.

"Who's that?" asked Slim.

"Oh, sorry Sir, my name is Sam Marsh."

"*The* Sam Marsh. You're big news!"

"Yes it seems so Sir."

"Well, it's very nice to be speaking with you Sam, and may I say how sorry I was to hear about your mom and dad."

"It's alright, I didn't know them," replied Sam.

"Anyhow, as I was saying there is someone down there, some kind of undersea vessel."

"Do you think it's a sub, Slim?" asked Alfie.

"Nope, it's no sub, it's massive."

"What should we do, Slim," asked Alfie.

"We need someone to go down and take a look."

"Well if we send a sub down then they'll see it and scramble it, they wouldn't stand a chance." said Alfie.

"No, no a sub is no good here, it would be a complete waste of our time, and we would give ourselves away, which we ain't gonna do, we need to be real careful with this one. If they've got the technology to build this kind of undersea base and the power to scramble from such a distance then they have the technology to cause us major problems, and by 'we' I mean the world!"

"So what do you suggest, Slim?" asked Alfie.

"We're gonna send a small team of special ops boys down for a look, then depending on what we see we will have to formulate some kind of action plan."

"It's that serious?"

"Yup, sure is!"

"Have you got any SEALS close by?" asked Alfie.

"What're SEALS?" asked Spike, "A bit like Sea Lions?"

"No," tutted Sam "SEALS are the special operations men of the United States navy, they undertake all kind of undercover investigations and missions."

"Nope," continued Slim, "none your side of the pond, but I've just spoken with Admiral Berg up at Ramsund.."

"Old Stig?"

"Yup, and he can have some men over to you within the next couple of hours, he's gonna get them choppered in. They'll take a look at the area and go for a midnight swim, then we'll take it from there, OK?"

"The weather is not so great over here, Slim, it may be difficult to get out to the site."

"Don't worry, well leave it with them for the moment, Alfie."

"Great, we'll see what they come up with."

"OK Alfie, I gotta go, the old guy in the Oval Office will be shouting if I'm not over there in ten seconds."

"Will you brief him?"

"You betcha, speak later!" and with that the computer link went dead and Slim Easton was gone.

"Who's up at Ramsund, Alfie?" asked Sam

"At Ramsund? Oh yeah, the Marinejegerkommandoen, or MJK for short are based at Ramsund, it's their northern base."

"But who are these MJK?" asked Spike.

"Oh, sorry, they are part of the Norwegian special forces Spike, a bit like the American Navy SEALS, or the British Special Boat Squadron, or SBS."

"I thought it was SAS?" said a confused Spike.

"They're different Spike, they're the Special Air Service, the SBS are the navy's special forces section.

37) 19 October 2011, 2030.

Ramsund Special Forces Base, Northern Norway.

The Ramsund naval base was 85 kms due east of Svolvaer over on mainland Norway. Based in the small coastal town of Ramsund with barely three hundred residents the base dominates the surrounding area and one of the most important groups of residents at the base were the MJK or Marinejegerkommandoen. Set up in the early 1950's the MJK is based in two locations, at Ramsund and also at the Haakonsvern Navy base in Bergen, further south. MJK like the British SBS and the US Navy SEALS specialise in unconventional types of warfare, in serious and often top secret missions. They came to the public attention in the 1970's when Norwegian North Sea oil production started in earnest. The vast profits of the oil business also attracted the attention of people who wanted to interfere with the industry, it attracted the interests of terrorist groups from around the world. The MJK were hugely successful in countering this new and dangerous threat.

Although not nearly as well known as their British and American cousins the MJK have developed a reputation for excellence, for creating and maintaining high standards and for being in great demand for situations all around the world.

Tonight Admiral Stig Berg's after dinner game of chess with his wife was interrupted by a very special person, by the President of the United States' National Security Advisor, Slim Easton, no less. Easton had called five minutes earlier and once again the phone in Stig's lounge tinkled.

"Berg!" said the Admiral picking up the phone, not wasting a single minute he'd been in touch with the base and put his men on 'action stations'. He'd got his boots and raincoat on and was ready for the four hundred metre sprint from his house over to the base, even at 64 years old and even in the driving wind and torrential rain he expected to make the base in under one minute ten seconds.

"Hi Stig, Slim here."

"Hello Slim, any further news?"

"I've told Alfie you'll chopper some men in within the next two hours and you'd be looking to get down for a dive before midnight. Is this possible?"

"Conditions are bad here Slim, it's a bad, bad storm, no ships are going to sea and any still out there," Stig paused looking out of the window at the pouring rain, "well, heaven help them, that's all I can say."

"My intelligence tells me that this may be something that affects not only the national security of Norway, but the entire world. If it is at all possible I want someone out there to take a look Stig, got me?"

"I understand, Sir," replied Admiral Berg. As the chief of the elite special operations unit here all of his men were highly trained, super soldiers, they formed part of a tight knit team, they were all good friends as well as colleagues and they were all the Admiral's friends. He didn't like taking risks with their lives, "we'll get choppered over Sir, I'll go personally, if we can't get a pilot crazy enough to take us I'll fly the bird myself!"

"Good man, Stig, keep me posted!"

Stig Berg put the phone down and shouted to his wife who was in the kitchen.

"Just going out darling! I might be late, don't wait up!"

"Be careful, Stig!" she replied.

"It's my middle name!" he shouted as he slammed the door shut behind him and sprinted off towards the Operations Room.

It took the admiral 69 seconds to get from his house to the team's Operations Room. When he entered the room he paused briefly to check his time and only looked up when everyone started laughing at him. In the MJK everyone was very informal, nobody used ranks when addressing each other and no one used the word "Sir".

"What?" said Stig looking up.

"Well, what time did you do?" asked Captain Morten Rudd, Stig's number two at the base.

"One minute and nine seconds!" grinned Stig.

"Not bad, one second faster than yesterday, Stig?"

"When you're as old as me, Mort, you'll take a one second improvement, believe me!"

Stig walked to the front of the room, at his request Morten had assembled a small team of six men, which added to the two of them meant that this would be a very sleek operation.

"OK guys, we've got ourselves a nice job for a rain soaked, windswept evening in the arctic circle, a dive down to the Røst Reef!"

"What? Tonight?" muttered the men.

"Yeah, yeah, I know, the conditions are far from ideal but we got ourselves something of an intruder."

"Where?" asked Morten.

"At the bottom of the ocean!"

"At the bottom of the ocean?" replied Morten as the rest of the men muttered the same response.

"Yep."

"What is it? A sub? A Russian sub or something?" asked Martin Pedersen, one of the youngest of the commandos at just twenty seven years old.

"Nope, Martin, nothing like that," Stig paused, "to be quite honest with you, we just don't know what it is down there. OK, I'll start from the beginning. This morning a mini sub was taking a dive off the Røst Reef, after a while they discovered an old wreck."

"That's nothing unusual," said Martin.

"No, not unusual at all, but if you'll just zip it for a second, I'll tell you the story! We haven't got time for interruptions so if you can please leave your questions for later I'll finish what I was saying!"

"Sorry, Chief!" replied Martin Pedersen sheepishly.

"OK, so they discovered this wreck, the wreck of a sub called the Helsmfjord, Morten will explain what he's found out about her in a moment. Just after finding the wreck they decided to surface and it was while they were coming up that a funny thing happened, they were scrambled!"

"Scrambled?" repeated a couple of the men.

"Yep, scrambled, their power went off and all the systems went down. Anyway, they managed to surface and luckily for us when they did this computer whizz kid who was with the party took the CPU from the mini sub and analysed it."

Stig Berg paused for breath.

"When he took a closer look he discovered where this scrambling signal had come from, and was able to give our American friends some interesting information. Anyway, I've just had a call from a top level colleague and they are taking this threat really seriously. Obviously they don't have any people over here that are able to go and take a look so he gave me a call."

"So we're going over there this evening?" asked Pedersen.

"Just as soon as we can get our kit together. There is not much more that I can add to that explanation, we really need to go and take a look, see what's down there. Any questions?"

Everyone shook their heads.

"OK, get your kit together boys, we're going for a swim!"

"We won't get a chopper pilot crazy enough to fly tonight Stig!" said Morten.

"Nope!" chuckled the Admiral cheekily "I know that, that's why you've got Uncle Stig flying you tonight children!"

38) 19 October 2011, 21.00. The Royal Villa.

As soon as he knew that the Norwegian special forces men were coming over to take a look at the reef Sam had an idea. He'd read a lot about special forces missions, he knew that stealth was the main priority, they must not get found out. In this case, nobody knew what the result of getting discovered would be. He just shuddered at what might happen. Nobody even knew who or what it was sitting at the bottom of the ocean with the ability to scramble passing ships or subs.

He left the others sat around Spike's computer discussing what might happen, but Sam always liked to be busy, to be doing something. He knew he could help in some way. His inventing skills could help the men from the MJK. He rushed down to his workshop and bolted the door behind him. He didn't want to be disturbed, he had important work to do and he had to work fast. He reckoned he had one hour maximum to get everything finished, tested and ready for use.

Sam plugged his laptop into the power and logged on. Whilst it was warming up he unlocked the store room door and started dragging two old sofas through to the workshop. They were very heavy but he somehow managed to drag them in. He pulled onto a pair of makeshift weighing scales and he measured them carefully. Returning to his laptop he fed the information into the special programme.

"How much will they weigh?" he thought, Sam thought that the men would be heavier than normal people, he took a guess at a maximum of 120 kilos, that should be ample.

So in went all the figures and after clicking on the enter button, the programme gave him just the exact amount of thrust he would need to fly two men out to the reef. He knew the rocket sofas could fly low, under any radars, he knew they would be small enough not to be detected and he knew they would get them there quickly, in maybe just one minute. He knew that speed would be really important to the soldiers.

Sam strapped on the biggest thrusters that he'd built and stuck the fuel tanks on to the back. Quickly he sewed the safety straps onto the material and finally he poured in the fuel, which would mix together when he wanted it to, right before take-off. They would have one hour's flying time and he knew that was more than enough.

The only two problem facing Sam was firstly, convincing the others that this was the best way to get out there, and secondly convincing someone that flying a rocket sofa wasn't the craziest idea in the whole, wide world!

39) 19 October 2011, 21.46. The gardens of the Royal Villa, Svolvaer.

At precisely fourteen minutes to ten the howling gale that was lashing the west coast of Norway was added to by the powerful engines of the Bell 412SP Helicopter coming in from the east.

Perfectly camouflaged, it had flown low all the way from Ramsund. It circled twice looking for the lights that Svend and Odd had laid out on the big lawn then it dropped down and landed. As the rotor blades gradually slowed down the doors were flung open and men dressed completely in black were getting out and unloading bags and bags of kit.

Last to get out was the pilot, who left the unloading to the others. Still keeping his head ducked down he jogged over to the house.

"Alfie!"

"Stig! How're you doing old friend?"

"Still working hard, how about you?"

"Oh, painting and sculpting, and a bit of diving," Alfie winked at Stig who laughed.

"Yeah so I'd heard, found us a bit of a troublemaker have you, Alfie?"

"Well I hope not, but when Slim took a look, he was quite keen to find out exactly what's down there."

"Well I've got three boys, led by Morten who are going down to have a look around but I'm really worried about how we're going to get over to the reef."

"Yeah, I'd been thinking about that too, the sea is just far too stormy to go over in a boat and I think you may attract the visitors attention if you take the chopper."

Just at that moment Sam came out of his workshop to see what all the noise was.

"Hi," said Sam quietly.

"Sam, Sam, come here, meet my friend Stig Berg. Stig this is Sam Marsh, you might have heard about him?"

"Sam Marsh? Of course I've heard of him," he smiled as he shook Sam's hand, Sam was a little in awe of the big MJK man, "it's a very small community around here, everyone knows everyone else and no one can have a secret."

"Hello," said Sam quietly, "I might know how you can get out to the reef really quickly and with very little fuss."

"You do?" said Stig, "go on then Sam, tell us, at the MJK we're always open to new ideas."

Sam cleared his throat and then blurted it straight out, "I've built a special rocket chair!"

"A rocket chair?" Alfie was about to laugh but Stig most certainly wasn't.

"You built a what, Sam?"

"A rocket chair Sir, well actually a rocket sofa, and I've actually built two of them!"

"Rocket sofas?" Alfie was still grinning, but wasn't when Stig nudged him.

"I would like to see them please Sam, is that possible?"

"Yes, sure."

Sam led the way to his workshop and everyone else, people from the house and all the MJK men started following.

"No!" said Stig abruptly, "just us."

Alfie continued to follow them, but Stig turned to him

"Just us two please Alfie, can you give us five?"

"Ja sure," said Alfie walking back to the house. He also knew Morten well and went to talk with him.

When Sam opened the door of his workshop and flicked the lights on, Stig was gobsmacked "You *have* built a rocket sofa!" he grinned.

"Yes, yes I have, Sir."

"Stig, please call me Stig. So how do you know they work, have you tested them?"

"I've tested the chair and I've tested the model, everything is the same about the sofas only bigger."

"Yeah, for sure!"

"Would you like to see the model fly, Stig?"

"Yeah, why not."

Sam, rushed over to the model and strapped his action man into the seat. He grabbed the remote control and turned the model on.

"Three, two, one, blast off!"

The model shot into the air, Sam expertly steered it around the workshop, over obstacles and under obstacles, this way and that, back and forth.

"It works!" shouted Stig over the noise.

"Yeah!" said Sam, "Have you seen enough?"

"Yeah!"

Sam brought the model in to land and then turned it off. They both felt like they'd gone deaf after all the noise.

"So?" asked Sam.

"I like it!"

"Do you want to use it?"

"Who's going to fly them?"

"I'll fly one and I need someone else to fly the second."

"We can't let you fly one of these Sam, it's too dangerous."

"We've not got the time to teach anyone else to fly them, can any of the other men fly?"

"No, just me," replied Stig.

"Then it's me flying one and you flying the other Stig!"

Sam didn't see the glint of excitement in Stig's eye. He couldn't wait to get strapped into one of these flying sofas. He couldn't believe he was about to do something so dangerous, so absurd, so crazy. How on earth would he explain all this to his men, they'd keel over in fits of laughter!

40) 19 October 2011, 22.30. Rocket Sofa's!

The men of the MJK all trusted Admiral Stig Berg's judgment completely. He was well known for his crazy ideas but as long they'd known him, he'd always got it right. Flying rocket sofas might seem like a crazy idea but if Stig said it would work, then it would work!

The sofas had been carried out on to the lawn, well away from the parked chopper.

"How are we going to be able to see in the dark?" asked Sam.

"Night vision goggles, here, try these on for size." replied Morten handing him a pair.

Sam tried the pair on and, all of a sudden, he could see, it looked a bit strange but he could see clearly even though it was pitch dark out to sea.

"Wow, these are great!" said Sam.

"Can you see, Sam?" asked Morten.

"Yeah."

"Can you see your control stick?"

Sam had used an old car gear stick as the control stick, he'd attached a simple dial that increased or decreased the speed. They were the only two controls on the rocket sofa.

Sam's heart was pumping as he pulled on a special flying suit with a life jacket and a MJK helmet. He really felt fantastic, terrified but so excited to be using one of his inventions for a really important mission.

"OK!" shouted Stig and the four men that had been selected for the dive walked slowly over to the sofas. They were walking like ducks because they had huge special ops flippers on their feet. They were wearing special black wetsuits and they were carrying hi tech boards that had tiny on-board computers which would tell them exactly where they were and where the wreck was. It would also allow them to broadcast on a special undetectable radio every move that they made as they swam down to the reef and then back towards the land. When they got back to land they would be met be a Land Rover on the beach.

The divers strapped themselves into the sofas. If they had have been going in the daylight and if anybody would have been watching it would been like a scene out of a comedy movie. But this was not a movie and it certainly was not a comedy, everybody was deadly serious.

When the men were ready Sam sat down between then and strapped himself in, on the other sofa Stig did the same.

"Radio check!" said Stig's voice in Sam's earphones.

"Check!" replied Sam.

"OK, prepare for take off!"

"All systems ready, Stig!"

"OK on my count, three, two, one, blast off!"

The sofas soared into the sky. It took a couple of seconds for Stig to get used to the controls but as he was an experienced pilot this took no time at all.

"OK, Stig?" asked Sam.

"OK."

"Sam to base, are you receiving me?"

"Loud and clear!" replied Alfie.

"OK Sam, can you see your compass and watch?" asked Stig as they circled around the villa.

"I can see them."

"OK, let's head due west for twenty seconds, then north for five and then south west for twenty, I've got a GPS monitor and when we get over the wreck I will tell you."

"OK!"

"Let's go!"

Exactly at the same time both rocket sofas zoomed off due west. Twenty seconds later they turned north for a further five seconds, then south west for the last twenty.

"We're here Sam, go in low and circle."

"OK!"

"OK, men unbuckle yourselves, on my count of three you're away, good luck, stay silent, stay undetected and we'll pick you up in about two hours time on one of the beaches of the islands."

"OK!" the men all answered at the same time.

"OK! Three, two, one, jump!"

The men all jumped at exactly the same time and plopped gently into the water as the sofas headed back to Svolvaer, retracing the exact path that they had taken on the outward journey. Within a couple of seconds they had disappeared into the stormy night as the divers silently dived down to the reef.

41) 19 October 2011, 22.45. The Røst Reef

Once under the water, the special forces divers placed their right arms over their neighbours shoulder to lock them with their colleague and with their left they held on to their special, computer boards. Taking slow, long powerful kicks, they automatically counted every single kick as they dropped down towards the place where the wreck lay. With the help of their underwater night vision goggles they could see clearly. Around the reef the waters were very turbulent and they struggled to stay joined together.

"Anders," said Martin through the intercom, "did you see that?"

"No, what?"

"That glint of silver over there?"

"No, I saw nothing."

"Look it's there again, it's just over at the other side of the wreck."

"I see it!" said Morten, "get down behind the coral, radio silence."

The four divers huddled together bracing themselves against the strong tidal surges that tried to bash them into the reef and got down out of sight of the silver object.

The divers watched, amazed as the long sleek shape zoomed around the wreck of the sixty year old submarine. It looked like a man, but a very, very tall thin man, but it swam like a dolphin. It was perfectly suited to swimming and it turned quickly and expertly around the wreck. It seemed to be making a record of everything about the wreck. As they watched in silence another of the silver creatures joined the first. It too was investigating the wreck, very, very carefully.

Suddenly they looked at each other, the men thought they'd been detected but the silver creatures must have been communicating that their work on the Helmsfjord was done. Quickly they shot off away from the wreck, away from the reef and out towards the open ocean.

"Follow them!" ordered Morten in nothing more than a whisper.

The divers moved as one, slowly, purposefully through the ocean, following the creatures.

"They're going deep, I don't think we can follow them much further Chief," noted Anders.

"They're slowing down, their base must be around here somewhere really close," replied Morten determined to follow the creatures to their base.

Suddenly the silver shapes ducked down.

"What the.....?"

Through the dark, murky deep water they saw it, a gigantic starfish shaped underwater construction. Its lights were dim at this distance but it was clearly a base. There were four enormous submarines moored against its long legs. The silver creatures went towards the base and straight inside.

Morten took some photos on the camera that was built into his board and then turned to the others.

"Quick, let's get out of here!" he said, "double back, complete radio silence, let's get home and tell the Chief about this."

42) 20 October 2011, 02.00. The Royal villa.

No one was sleeping at the royal villa tonight. Everyone was up helping with the mysterious situation. Sam and Stig had zoomed straight back to the villa grounds after dropping the divers off. Sam, who was well used to the rocket systems had landed smoothly and gently on the lawn in exactly the right place but Stig had landed very hard. He overshot the lawn and smacked right into a huge piece of hedge just next to the front of the villa. He'd been lucky though he'd only broken his thumb.

Straight away Stig had set up a control room in the lounge and Jorunn, Freyer, and Jenny were making sandwiches and hot drinks for the men.

At precisely two am, Odd walked back into the villa, followed by the four soggy divers who were huddled in fluffy pink bath towels.

"I found some friends of yours washed up on the beach Stig!"

"Fantastic, thanks Odd, everything OK, fellas?"

"No, everything is not OK Chief," replied a worried looking Morten.

"Why, what did you find?"

"OK, where shall I start?" said Morten being passed a cup of hot chocolate, "Thanks. Well, after you dropped us off, we dived down to the wreck and got there fine, no problems at all, but while we were there Martin saw something out of the corner of his eye, at first we thought he was seeing things but then I saw it too."

"What was it?" asked Jenny, handing around the drinks to the divers.

"Heaven knows!" replied Morten, "they looked like men, long silver men."

"What do you mean long silver men?" asked Stig, "did you see Martians?"

Morten gave his Chief a hard stare, "They were easily three metres tall, and they swam just like dolphins or seals, just like underwater mammals."

"What were they doing?" asked Sam.

"Not quite sure, but we think they were taking measurements of the wreck of the Helmsfjord."

"Really?" said Stig.

"We think so, anyway after a couple of minutes they turned and swam out into the ocean, so we followed them."

"We thought they were going to go too deep for us," said Anders.

"But just as we were thinking about turning back we saw it."

"Saw what?" asked Stig.

"The base!"

"The base?"

"Yeah, it was like nothing any of us have seen before, massive it was, looked like a giant starfish, maybe one thousand metres from the tips of one leg to the tip of the others. It was huge and there were massive submarines docked against some of the legs."

"How many?" asked Alfie.

"Four. Look I took a photo of the base. Anyone got a USB cable and I'll put it on to that laptop?"

"Here's one," said Spike passing a short, black cable over.

Morten plugged the cable into the laptop and then into his diver's board. After a couple of minutes the photo came up on the screen. Everyone gasped in surprise.

"Good grief!" gasped Alfie.

"I've never seen anything like it before!" agreed Stig, "Alfie get Slim on the line straight away and get him to dial into Spike's laptop."

"I'm on it!" said Alfie dialling Slim in the USA, where it was after ten pm. But everyone was pleased to discover that Slim was still wide awake and at his desk.

"Hi, Alfie, Hi, Stig, Hi, kids and everyone else!" he voice boomed out of the phone speaker.

"Hi Slim!" replied Sam, Spike and Jenny.

"OK! What's going on there?"

"Slim, can you dial into Spike's computer?" said Alfie.

"I'm on it now.." there was a long silence, then he spoke again, "how big is that thing?"

This time it was Morten who spoke, "Maybe about one thousand metres from tip to tip, Sir."

"Is that Morten?"

"Yes, Sir."

"Hi. The subs, how big would you say they are, Morten?"

"I would say 250 metres long, I've never seen anything like them before. Easily the biggest subs that I've ever seen."

"Could they be Russian?" asked Stig.

"Nope, not Russian, definitely not Chinese, they're years behind us and from the look of that set up these people are years ahead of us!"

"What do you think, Slim?" asked Alfie.

"Give me two minutes I'll take some advice from a man who knows about these things, I'll show him this picture. Don't go away!"

It was five minutes before they heard from Slim Easton again. Everyone was sat nervously huddled around the blazing wood burning stove. The divers had gone and showered and got changed out of their wet suits.

"Hi y'all!" Slim's voice boomed out of the computer's speakers, "are you still awake over there?"

"We're all awake!" replied Alfie, "What do you think, Slim?"

"Well I now know what it is and who owns it."

"You do? Well, go on then!" said Stig.

"It's called Unterwasserwelt," said Slim.

"Underwater World!" translated Freyer quietly.

Everyone looked at her.

"I speak some German," she hugged Sam tightly as Slim continued.

"Right, Underwater world, it is a privately owned state of the art underwater military base owned by.."

"The Company!" answered Freyer again.

Everyone stared at her in disbelief.

"A good guess maybe?" she said.

"Well Mrs.....?" said Slim.

"Becken, Freyer Becken, I'm Sam Marsh's great grandmother."

"Well Mrs Becken, seeing as you seem to know so much would you like to tell the rest of them who is in charge of The Company?"

"A man called Herr Krater, Professor Eric Krater."

"He is my great grandfather!" said Sam almost silently.

Everyone sat stunned for a few moments but it was the National Security Advisor who broke the silence.

"Is there anything else you two want to tell us about Herr Eric Krater and The Company?"

"I don't know anything else about him," replied Sam shrugging his shoulders.

"Mrs Becken?"

"I knew him during the war, I haven't seen him for over sixty five years Mr Easton. I got an investigator to find out a little about him a few years ago, more out of curiosity than anything else, I suppose. I discovered then that he was in charge of The Company, a secretive organisation that owns large parts of many companies all around the world, a company that spends tens of billions of dollars on research, that is primarily involved in the manufacture of high tech military hardware. Further than that I decided to take the advice of my investigator."

"Which was?"

"Keep well away from him because people get hurt if they get too close to him. He was warned off and he suggested to me that we close our little investigation."

"Mrs Becken, do you have any idea why he may be trying to recover the submarine, the Helmsfjord."

Freyer gulped.

"Mrs Becken, it may be vitally important to world peace."

"Go on Gran if there's anything you know, tell them!" urged Sam.

"He is a genius you know and also an engineer, his speciality is rocket propulsion, when we split up he was working on a new fuel source, he was very excited about it but it was top secret. It was something that he said would win them the war in six months. He said it would change the world! He told me that he and his colleagues had drawn up one set of plans! They'd conducted a lot of tests up near the Northern Cape, but they had to send the plans to Berlin for another scientist to resolve something they couldn't work out. It was all very hush, hush."

"Do you think those plans could be in that sub, Mrs Becken."

"I'm almost one hundred per cent certain that they are on that submarine Mr Easton. Herr Krater does not waste his time, effort or money on wild goose chases."

"Do you think he was correct, what he said about the fuel?"

"I wouldn't bet against him, Mr Eastman, he has built Unterwasserwelt as you see, something powerful must be fuelling that, after all, have you got anything as impressive as that underwater?"

"No Maam, nothing nearly half as good as that base, I think we ought to take this very seriously, we need to stop Krater getting to those plans before we all regret it!"

43) 20 October 2011, 6 am. Unterwasserwelt.

"Everything is ready Herr Krater," said the feeble voice of the ancient Profesor Jahnke.

"The divers have confirmed that the safe is intact, Jahnke?"

"Yes, Sir, it is intact and in a place where they can get to it very easily."

"Order them to open the Helmsfjord and to retrieve the safe, send eight of them, that should be enough to bring it to us."

"Yes, Sir."

Krater stared out through the window in his underwater office and sighed deeply, they were almost there, decades of work were finally drawing to a satisfactory conclusion, "We have come such a long way Jahnke," he said as the Professor was almost at the door.

He turned around and stared back at Krater, "A long way but in a very long time Professor Krater," he replied.

"Yes, but Jahnke my old friend, soon we will travel a long way in a very short time!"

"Aye, aye, Professor Jahnke," said Gurt Zimmermann in the torpedo room, "I'll prepare eight for launch immediately."

The portly Zimmermann wobbled over to what seemed to be a large storage cabinet of some kind and pulled the sliding door back, inside were twelve long misty plastic tubes stood on their end from floor to ceiling. He keyed in a code, stood back and waited.

"Robo Divers one to eight report for duty!" he said clearly.

The first eight tubes started clearing and slowly sliding down to reveal a motionless silver diver. Diver one carefully stepped out of the tube, followed by number two and so on until all eight were out and awaiting instructions. When all eight robodivers were ready, the first diver spoke to Zimmermann.

"Robo divers one to eight reporting for duty sir!"

"Open tubes one to eight and prepare for dive!"

"What are our orders, Sir?"

"Swim to the wreck of the Helmsfjord, enter the submarine, locate the safe, retrieve the safe, bring it back here to Unterwasserwelt."

"Aye, aye, Sir!" said the robot climbing into the first tube.

All the others did the same. When they were all in a tube, Gurt Zimmermann checked that they had loaded themselves properly. He knew that they always did everything correctly but through force of habit the old sailor like to check things personally, after all if there was a problem it could backfire on him, literally! He closed the tubes and keyed in the launch command code.

One by one the divers were blasted into the dark, cold ocean and out towards the wreck.

"Commander Reich from torpedo room!" called Gurt Zimmermann on the intercom.

"Reich here, go ahead Gurt."

"All tubes launched, Sir."

"Well done, Gurt."

The two elderly professors had joined Commander Reich on the bridge.

"Approaching the wreck," came the inhuman voice of Robo Diver one over the loudspeakers.

"Approach with care, number one," replied Reich.

"Aye, Sir. Three and four are now cutting the hull, evidence of severe corrosion is apparent, they have cut a hole. We are all entering the Helmsjord."

"Be very careful!" called Krater nervously.

"Aye, Sir. Extreme care being observed!" replied the robot, "Team now entering the bridge."

"It's in a small room just to the side of the bridge!" shouted Krater.

"We have found the room, we have located the safe, number seven is testing for damage."

Everyone nervously held their breath

"The safe has been opened already," reported the diver.

"What!" shouted Krater, "it can't have been, you checked yesterday!"

"The safe has been opened recently!"

"What? Who could have done such a thing, who knew it was there?"

"Number eight has detected signs of human life moving away from the wreck. What are our orders?"

"Get out of there and follow them!" shouted Krater.

"Aye, aye, Sir!"

The robodivers carefully moved out of the wreck and out into open water. Free from the confines of the ancient submarine immediately they set off after the intruders who were heading straight for the surface.

44) 20 October 2011, 6.10. The surface above the Røst Reef.

Morten and Anders had just reached the surface. They took off their breathing masks and looked around for their lift which was nowhere to be seen. On Morten's front was a satchel in which were the plans that they had just got from the safe on the wreck of the Helmsfjord. It had taken them almost an hour to find and open the safe and now they were exhausted.

"Where are they?" asked a worried Anders.

"Don't know."

Suddenly from the west they heard a loud noise coming their way fast, getting louder and louder all the time.

"Here they come!" called Morten, "Stig's always late, and now he's getting Sam into his bad habits!"

As the weird looking rocket sofas zoomed low over the water the pilots threw down ropes. When they had planned this pick up they knew it would be dangerous but they had decided that they couldn't risk using the chopper or a boat in case the enemy discovered what they'd done and scrambled them. The risk of this causing a terrible accident was just too great. The rocket sofas were so simple that scrambling wouldn't affect them, they had no on-board computers and all the electrics were so basic. They were basically fool proof.

"Go in low, Sam!" ordered Stig, "I'll take the first run and then you can take the second if we need one. In case of any problems, I'll circle around and get ready for another go. What is the fuel situation?"

"We've got a lot of fuel," shouted Sam confidently, he was really getting to like this flying business.

As they'd agreed Stig was the first to attempt a pick up, he flew low towards the divers nearly deafening them, the rope was plunged into the water. Closer, closer it got to them. They lunged for the rope but it missed them by a couple of metres.

Sam was next. He followed Stig in low and looked down to make sure his rope was in the water. They were flying so fast they had to be really careful where the rope went. If they got it wrong they could hit one or even both of the men with it and badly hurt them. Sam was getting closer and closer, he was there! Morten desperately reached across but couldn't quite get hold of the rope.

"I'm going in again, Sam!"

Stig readjusted his flight path and went even lower, just skimming the surface of the waves which were still very high from the storm that was still raging.

"Don't go too low Stig, or you'll hit the water!" shouted Sam.

It was too late Stig had skimmed the water and the force of even such a small impact combined with the speed he was travelling sent him scuttling into the sky. He fought desperately to control the sofa, using his years of experience to good effect.

"I'm OK, I'm OK!" he called breathlessly, "you give it another go, Sam!"

Sam decided he wouldn't go in as low as Stig had, he couldn't risk hitting the water because he knew he wasn't strong enough to control the sofa if it got into trouble. He got into position, his height was just right, his speed perfect, the rope was down in the water. They'd caught it! Both of them had caught hold of the rope! He could see that they'd clicked their security grips in place. They were safe. Suddenly the two divers felt really heavy, strangely heavy.

"What is it, Stig?" shouted Sam over the radio, "Why's it so heavy?" Sam was really worried.

"You've picked up something else on you line too fisherman Sam," replied Stig, "don't worry, you can't do anything about it, leave it to Anders."

At the split second that Morten and Anders had stretched out for the rope Anders had felt something grab him around the ankles. A hand with a vice like grip! When he looked down he got the shock of his life. There was a long silvery man attached to his leg! As they flew into the sky the man's grip didn't seem to fail one bit, in fact it got painfully tighter!

"Stig, one of those things has got a hold of my leg?" he called on the radio.

"Try and smash it off with your divers board."

Anders whacked and whacked the Robodiver but it wouldn't let go. It was locked on.

"It's starting to cut into my leg, I can't stop it!"

Stig decided there was only one thing for it, he had to do something.

"Keep heading for home Sam, I'm gonna fly in and whack it!"

"What?"

Using expert flying skills, Stig pulled right back on his control stick, coming up at Sam's sofa really quickly from underneath slicing through the air like a razor sharp knife! He shot past the bottom of Anders' leg and whacked the robot on the head, knocking him out cold.

"Thanks, Chief!" called Anders, "he still on there, his grip appears to be locked but he's not cutting my leg anymore."

45) 20 October 2011, 6.25. The Bridge of Unterwasserwelt.

Herr Krater was incandescent with rage. His face was bright purple, Commander Reich thought he was going to keel over. Krater was banging his fist down, and kicking things. He even kicked a robot off its chair he was so furious.

"How dare they steal my plans?" he shouted, "*my* plans, *my* plans!"

"I can order Gurt Zimmermann to launch the Amphibibots," suggested Reich cautiously.

"What?"

"The Amphibibots, I can order Gurt Zimmermann to launch them."

"But we don't know where they've taken the plans? They could have gone miles. It would be a fruitless search."

"At least we can try."

"Very well, Reich."

46) 20 October 2011, 6.35. The Royal villa.

Stig suggested that he land first and help Sam land the men and the prisoner. This time he landed in exactly the right spot and without crashing. He was getting to like flying the strange sofa flying machine!

"Quick!" he called to the others, "Sam's got an extra passenger! Get the big inflatable, men, get it pumped up real quick, we've not got much time!"

The commandos sprang to life and pulled the giant inflatable quickly into position. With amazing speed they set up the compressor and within thirty seconds the inflatable was ready.

"Sam, can you hear me?" Stig spoke on his radio.

Sam was circling round and round the villa, going as slowly as he could.

"Yeah, I can hear you, Stig," he replied.

"The inflatable's ready, fly low over it and when I tell you cut the rope, OK?"

"OK!"

Sam did as he was told, expertly flying low and as slowly as possible towards the target.

"Sam, nearly there, OK?"

"OK!"

"Three, two, one, cut!"

The rope was cut at exactly the right time and all three passengers dropped on to the massive cushion. Quickly Anders and Morten rolled away to safety, but the robot just remained in the middle of the target motionless.

Sam landed and Jenny, Freyer and Jorunn went to see if he was OK.

"Yeah, yeah I'm fine," he said pulling his helmet off, "what is that thing?"

Everyone was crowded around the silver robot man watching it carefully. Just as Sam and the others got to them it started making noises, it was coming round.

"It's waking up!" called Spike.

"It might be dangerous!" shouted Jenny.

Quickly Stig pulled his helmet off and whacked the robot diver over the head with it.

"Not any more!" he grinned.

"Wow!" said Spike.

"Yeah, you don't get to become an admiral without a spot of quick thinking every now and again!"

47) 20 October 2011, 6.45. The Bridge of Unterwasserwelt.

"I have a trace, Sir!" called out a robot who was trying to find out where the missing robo diver was.

"A trace?"

"Aye, Sir."

"Herr Krater, we've got em!"

"Launch back up, launch everything we have! Forget about the Amphibibots! Launch the cavalry. Use whatever force you need to get those plans back. Whatever! I must have those plans! Bulldoze the entire Lofoten Islands if necessary!"

48) 20 October 2011, 7.15. The Royal villa.

Stig had a nasty feeling that bringing the robot back to the royal villa wasn't such a good idea. He was suspicious of the technology, he knew wherever it had come from, whoever owned it would use it to trace them, to trace the plans. He knew they were coming so he'd been straight on the phone to Slim as soon as he landed.

"What's that noise?" asked Freyer.

"What noise?" replied Stig.

"It's coming from the sea!" called Jenny.

"Look!" shouted Sam, "the sea's boiling!"

Stig turned and looked at the sea, it was true, it was bubbling furiously.

"Get inside the villa, get down into the cellar, it's a fortified bunker, it can withstand a nuclear attack!"

"I'm staying!" shouted Sam.

"No, you're not!" replied Odd grabbing and picking him up and running for the house with him tucked under his arm.

"Everyone inside except soldiers!" called Stig, "full action stations men!" he shouted. He was deadly serious now.

The commandos were incredibly well prepared with mobile missile launchers and rocket propelled grenade launchers apart from their normal weapons.

In the distance they could just see the waves parting and the bubbling getting louder and fiercer, then they could hear them, hear the strange machines, except it wasn't wheels or tanks they could hear, it was more like footsteps! Gigantic monstrous footsteps!

49) 20 October 2011, 8.20 am. The bridge of "The big stick".

The USS aircraft carrier the Theodore Roosevelt, known affectionately to the United States Navy as "The big stick!" and its carrier battle group which consisted of supporting ships and submarines was moving into position. They had just been joined by the older USS Enterprise's carrier battle group. Both had been put on red alert the evening before by the United States National Security Advisor, Slim Easton.

Quickly and purposefully they had moved into a position west of the Lofoten Islands and now they were launching everything they had to defend their allies from this unknown enemy which they knew had a tremendous technological advantage over them. They were counting on the element of surprise, that and the sheer volumes of planes they would use. Within three minutes there were over one hundred aircraft in the air, spearheaded by the supersonic F/A-18E/F Super Hornet jets, all armed with armour piercing canons and various kinds of air to air missiles.

"Seek out and destroy the enemy before it destroys us!" were their orders. They had to work fast, before the enemy attempted to neutralize their systems. They knew that this was a real possibility.

50) 20 October 2011, 8.25. The Royal villa.

The seas around the villa were bubbling and bursting with activity, an alien invasion in a science fiction film.

The first the commandos saw of their enemy was when the giant metallic spider's heads rose up over the cliffs, scaling them as if they weren't even there!

"What on earth are they?" shouted Morten.

The men had quickly dug holes in the lawn, and they had got down well out of sight. In fact only their eyes and the tips of their weapons could be seen above the ground.

The round metal balls rose up into the air on long metal legs, eight of them on each spider, they were easily ten metres tall. More and more of the spiders appeared until the entire horizon was full of them. They thudded along menacingly, getting closer and closer.

"We can't wait any longer," shouted Stig, "Open fire!"

The commandos opened fire with everything they had, guns, grenades, missiles, everything, but although they hit their targets the weapons barely dinted the machines, which just kept on coming closer and closer.

Then the invaders opened fire. A terrible whooshing of laser beams fired from the front of their heads, they were cutting the villa down like it was made of cardboard.

"Fire!" shouted Stig again. Still the response was the same.

The lasers opened up again. Within ten seconds the royal villa was completely gone, and now they could see that they were aiming directly at the men in their bunkers!

Suddenly there was a different noise getting louder, a tremendous roar coming in from the sea. Skimming low over the sea the Super Hornets howled towards the spiders at a phenomenal speed, opening up with their armour piercing canons first. But the canons seemed to have little effect on the spiders thick skin and they merely turned and fired their lasers back at the aircraft. Most of the Super Hornets managed to take evasive action but one bird was hit, the pilot managing to eject before it crashed down into the sea and exploded. "Tell them to fire their sidewinder air to air missiles at their legs!" shouted a little voice from beside Stig.

When he twisted around it was Sam, his crash helmet firmly stuck on his head.

"Sam, what are you doing here?" shouted Stig, "It's dangerous!"

"I know! But just tell them before they all get shot down or scrambled! They haven't much time!"

Stig got on his radio straight away, "Stig to the Big Stick, Stig to the Big Stick, over!"

"Big Stick here, go ahead Stig!"

"Your boys are gonna get blown out of the sky unless you fire your sidewinders at their legs!"

"OK Stig we read you loud and clear, over!"

As the next wave of jets screamed in they did just as they were asked and fired their air to air sidewinder missiles at the legs of the spiders. The first missile missed and thundered into the cliffs, the next smashed into a set of metal legs, destroying the spider, another hit a leg and did the same. Wave after wave of jets launched missile after missile. The air was full of explosions. There were three jets that had been shot down but all the pilots managed to bail out. The brutal attack went on for half an hour but by the end of that time all of the spiders had been destroyed and nothing else was emerging from the ocean.

"I think we showed em, Sam!" smiled Stig breathing a sigh of relief.

51) 20 October 2011, 9.05. Unterwasserwelt.

On the bridge of Unterwasserwelt there was complete chaos, it had become very clear that their vast landing party was suffering terrible losses.

"I'm getting reports Herr Krater, Sir, that the entire attack force has been destroyed by the American aircraft," said Reich calmly.

"What?" screamed Krater, "The *entire* force?"

"Yes, Sir."

"How could they do that with those, those clockwork toy planes!"

"Maybe they're not as clockwork as you think!" mumbled Reich under his breath.

"What was that?" snapped Krater.

"Nothing, Sir, I suggest we retreat, we must preserve Unterwasserwelt, we do not want to get into a war with the entire US Navy's Atlantic fleet, not yet anyway."

"They are nothing compared to us!" raged Herr Krater.

"Maybe not, Sir, but they have vast numbers and enormous fire power," Reich paused, "Sir, I respectfully suggest we retreat into the deep Atlantic at full speed before they start coming after us as well!"

"Nonsense, launch the X boats! Destroy the carrier battle groups!"

"Sir, I suggest that this is very, very unwise!"

"Launch them!" screamed the old man, and with that he grabbed his old friend Professor Jahnke by the sleeve and led him out off the bridge.

"Launch the X boats! Attack the Carrier Battle groups!" ordered Reich reluctantly.

52) 20 October 2011, 10.00 am. At the remains of the Royal villa.

The villa was like a burning ember, it had been almost completely destroyed in the battle. Quickly all the commandos had leapt out of their dugouts and gone to free the others from the bunker.

"Sam! Sam!" cried Freyer hugging Sam, "Where did you disappear to? I've been so worried Sam, I thought you'd been killed!"

"No, I'm fine Oldemor, I really am."

"Is everyone OK down there?" called Stig down into the bunker.

"Yeah, we're all OK!" the group answered.

"We watched it all on the TV monitors, Stig," said Spike excitedly, "awesome battle mate!"

"Thanks."

"Is everyone up here OK?" asked Jorunn looking around at the devastation.

"Yeah, all present and correct!" laughed Stig.

"But what about the pilots that ejected?" asked Jenny, "Are they OK?"

"Yeah, all OK, they've been picked up by the choppers and are headed back to their carriers. They need to be checked out by the docs but they'll be fine, they train for this sort of thing."

"Ooh!" gasped Spike, pointing, "look at your chopper Stig, that's definitely not OK!"

Stig's shiny new helicopter was now just a smouldering pile of burnt out black metal.

"No! I loved that bird!" sighed the Admiral, "I bet they won't want to give me another one!"

"You do realise, Stig, that the underwater people will try and blow up the American ships now don't you?" stated Spike.

"Oh, no!" replied Stig picking up his phone.

"I can scramble them though if you can take me to the carriers, whilst I was in the bunker I've figured out a way of reversing the signal, I've even tested it out, it's fail safe!"

"OK, OK! Leave it with me...Stig to the Big Stick, over!" Stig was already on the radio, "Can you get a chopper over here straight away, we've got a whizz kid here who can save you a whole lot of time and make sure nobody gets hurt your side!"

"Will do, Stig, we sure like the sound of that, a chopper's on its way!"

53) 20 October 2011, 11.00 am.

The bridge of the USS Theodore Roosevelt.

Spike had rushed off the chopper and been led straight up to the bridge, at the top of the huge tower, of the immense Nimitz-class super-carrier, the USS Theodore Roosevelt (CVN-71). He'd been too busy to say hello to anyone as his mind was occupied with what he'd said he could do. He'd lied about it being tried and tested, it wasn't, it was a long shot, a real shot in the dark, but a long shot that could save thousands of lives. But the Americans were ready to fight the enemy if Spike should fail to scramble them.

"Here, come here!" shouted Stig who led him onto the vast and crowded bridge, "Permission to come onto the bridge, Sir, he shouted at the commanding officer, Admiral Jim Gordon.

"Permission granted!" replied the Admiral, "welcome aboard young man, I hope you can do what you say you can!"

"I'll try, Sir," replied Spike as he plugged his brand new Toshiba laptop in and fired it up, "Can I log onto to your system, Sir?" he asked looking up.

The Admiral looked carefully at Spike and Stig.

"Slim Easton has cleared him, Sir!" said Stig.

The Admiral nodded, "Well if it's OK with Slim, it's OK with me."

Spike quickly logged into the ship's IT system.

"Can you get me past the firewall, Sir?"

"Sure, I'm on it!" Gordon dialled a number and within five seconds Spike was allowed in by the firewall.

Quickly he set his programme up and then he hit "enter"!

"Admiral, we've picked up something on the sonar!" shouted the sonar man.

"How many of 'em?" snapped Gordon.

"Four submarines, Sir, big ones, moving real fast, they are headed our way. No wait.....!" the man stopped speaking and listened intently to his sonar, "er, that's strange Sir, they've all just stopped, they appear to be just floating, they don't seem to have any power," he listened some more, "now they're surfacing, Sir."

"Are they completely disabled?" asked the Admiral.

"They are, Sir, they are completely dead in the water."

"Send the destroyers over to pick up any crew, secure lines to the subs and tow them to shore, send a team onboard to make sure they are completely empty and powerless."

"They already are completely powerless, Sir!" said Spike confidently looking at his computer, "I've scrambled them!"

The destroyers got quickly over to the Xboats. When the men went on board however they discovered them completely empty. There were no crew members about. Nobody. The first man to board the ship was Captain Bill Swain.

"Admiral, there's nobody on board!"

"Nobody?"

"Not a single living soul, Sir!"

"On your way over did you see anyone bail out, Captain?"

"No, Sir." as the Captain and his small boarding party walked around the ship they were recording everything that they discovered. They walked on to the bridge.

"This is some fantastic submarine Sir!" he gasped, "What's that?" his attention was drawn to something moving just by the helm, which was strange because everything else, all the other systems were completely dead, it was a countdown and the numbers were at 9.35...9.34...9.33...9.32, "Oh no!" he yelled rushing back out of the bridge, "come on! Let's get out of here, get the ships away, don't worry about us, we'll catch up in the speed boats."

All the men got off the strange submarines as quickly as they could, fired up their speed boats and hurtled after the rapidly departing ships. The carriers were ten miles away so they were safe.

Inside the subs the timers counted down exactly at the same time. "7...6...5...4...3...2...1..nothing! No explosion nothing. Then suddenly a series of small holes blew in their hulls and they started sinking. Then with four huge booms they all exploded at the same time!

54) 20 October 2011, 12 noon. Deep beneath the sea.

As Unterwasserwelt silently moved deeper and deeper along the ocean floor into the northern ocean, first moving due west then changing her course to north, she was headed for the north pole, she would hide far beneath the freezing winter ice shelves and await further orders.

When Unterwasserwelt was at a safe distance from the US carrier battle groups Herr Krater boarded his own X boat and left without uttering a single word to anyone.

He was deep in concentration. This had been a mere hitch in his plans, he would overcome it, he always did. But his thoughts were focused mainly on three things, the plans that had been stolen from him, a woman called Freyer Becken and a boy called Sam Marsh. He was starting to piece together the jigsaw.

Krater had spies everywhere and his contacts on the Lofoten Islands had reported that a woman called Freyer Becken had arrived a couple of days earlier. At first he was shocked by this news. He remembered her clearly even though he had not seen her for over sixty five years. There would only be one reason why she would turn up out of the blue at the villa, the boy. He had to be her great grandson. His spies had taken pictures of them, pictures of the boy, and he nearly collapsed when he saw his picture. He looked just as he had done as a child. They could have been twins! From that moment he knew that the boy was his flesh and blood, this was something that scared him a lot. If he, a tired old man couldn't create and develop the anti matter fuel then he knew that the boy would be able to do the same, he was his great grandson after all. He must be a genius. All his family were.

He had to make contact with Sam Marsh. If he wouldn't join with him on his quest he would have to stop him developing it for someone else, for his Norwegian friends, for the British or maybe his new friends, the Americans! Krater would never let Sam Marsh work with anyone else!

55) 21 October 2011, 10 am. Alfie Blom's cottage.

Sam, Spike and Jenny came sprinting down the cliff steps down to Alfie's small hut which had amazingly survived the battle.

"Alfie!, Alfie!" they called.

"Ja, ja, I'm here, come in, out of the rain!" he shouted from inside.

Inside it was jam packed with paintings, weird gadgets, and lots of books, in the middle of the small lounge was a roaring wood burner, and the dogs were sprawled out in front of it fast asleep.

"Everything is alright then, Alfie?" asked Sam.

"Ja, no breakages at all. Are you settling in to the hotel?"

"I suppose," replied Sam.

"What's the matter Sam."

"It's just that house, the royal villa, it was my first real home, my mum and dad's home, and now it's gone!"

"Don't worry Sam, they'll build a new one, it'll look exactly the same."

"But it won't be the same though!"

"Look Sam, you don't need a building or objects to remember people, you remember them in your mind, in your thoughts. You've got Freyer and she's got you. You didn't have that a week ago did you?"

"No, no I didn't," said Sam brightening up.

Alfie turned to Spike and Jenny, "So, I bet you'll be ready to go home, after all this action?"

"No, it's not my home!" snapped Jenny.

"Jenny's coming back to visit for a month at Christmas," said Sam putting his arm around her and giving her a hug.

"And you Spike, are you coming over at Chrismas?"

"Me? No, I can't, I've got plans."

"Plans?"

"Yeah, I'm going on work placement with Admiral Gordon, on the Theodore Roosevelt."

"Really?"

"Yeah, for real, he was impressed with me and has asked me to work with their IT team on a special project. I can't tell you about it though, it's top secret!"

"Where did the plans go to, Alfie?" asked Sam.

"Oh, they're safe and sound, our friend Slim has them, don't worry about them."

"Alfie?"

"Yes Sam."

"You know that old jet ski in your hut?"

"Yes," said Alfie slowly.

"Can I buy it from you, I'm working on a new engine for them, I've got lots of ideas!"

"Sure, Sam, but no rocket engines this time!"

THE END

Sam Marsh will return in

"Sam Marsh and the battle of the cloudships"

"My grateful thanks goes to everyone on the beautiful Lotoften Islands who helped with the researching of this book, who provided reference books, information, material and personal accounts. Thank you for your patience with my endless questions."

Cover Illustration by Louisa Biggin

Printed in Great Britain
by Amazon.co.uk, Ltd.,
Marston Gate.